GOD Don't Like HATERS 3

By

Jordan Belcher

Felony Books, a division of Olive Group, LLC,
P.O. Box 1577, Belton, MO 64012

Copyright © 2019 by Jordan Belcher

This book is a work of fiction. Names, characters, places, and incidents are products of the author's imagination or are used fictitiously. Any resemblance to actual events or locales or persons living or dead is entirely coincidental.

All rights reserved. No part of this book may be reproduced in any form or by any means without the prior written consent of the Publisher, excepting brief quotes used in reviews.

ISBN-13: 9781731536303

Felony Books 1st edition January 2019

10 9 8 7 6 5 4 3 2 1

Manufactured in the United States of America

For information regarding special discounts for bulk purchases, please contact Felony Books at felonybooks@gmail.com.

Books by Felony Books

TOO REAL FOR FAKE LOVE
TOO REAL FOR FAKE LOVE 2
TRAP FEVER 1
TRAP FEVER 2
TRAP FEVER 3
RICO
RICO 2
RICO 3
RICO 4
O.P.P.
O.P.P. 2
O.P.P. 3
REVENGE IS BEST SERVED COLD
REVENGE IS BEST SERVED COLD 2
REVENGE IS BEST SERVED COLD 3
SCANDALS OF A CHI-TOWN THUG
HELL HAS NO FURY
HELL HAS NO FURY 2
RICH & PETTY
RICH & PETTY 2
RICH & PETTY 3
FREEDOM'S GAME
FREEDOM'S GAME 2
FREEDOM'S GAME 3
BESIDE EVERY THUG
BESIDE EVERY THUG 2
GWOP GANG
GWOP GANG 2
GWOP GANG 3
WHEN THE DIMES DROP

and more ...

www.felonybooks.com

Text **FELONY** to **77948**

And stay updated on all of Felony Books' *newest releases, free giveaways,* and *special promotions!*

CHAPTER 1

Sundi Ashworth
Manhattan, New York

I sat at the table looking down at the smartphone in my lap, as I waited for Thomas Dyer to show up. I was surfing The Site, scrolling by every post, not reading a thing, just scrolling away with my thumb—because I was nervous as hell sitting here alone. I was starting to think that Thomas wasn't going to show up, that he was on to me. *He knows I'm working with La'Renz,* I thought, as I finally looked up and scanned the upscale restaurant for his friendly face. *Why else wouldn't he be here? He knows ...*

"Refill?" the waiter asked me, appearing out of nowhere. He didn't give me a chance to answer. With a white cloth draped over his forearm, he bent slightly at the waist with the smallest, most accommodating smile—a sign of a seasoned Manhattan server—and filled my glass from a pitcher of icy tequila.

"Thank you, sir," I said.

His smile opened up perfectly. "You're very welcome, Ms. Ashworth." Then he was off, disappearing again.

I noticed that he didn't ask me if I was ready to order this time. It would've been repeat question number three. If he had asked, I would've said no again but this time I would've got up and left. I was tired of waiting. And I couldn't shake the feeling that Thomas was privy to my new role as a Taylor Music Group spy.

I sipped some of my flavorful alcohol, even though I'd had too much already.

"Hey, girl."

I was surprised by a man's hand on my bare shoulder, then Thomas Dyer was drawing his arms around me. I had wanted to stand up to embrace him, to give him my full body as a way to remind him that I was a longtime friend and hopefully lower his defenses, but he didn't give me a chance. He hugged me sitting.

Then he sat across me, his stomach bumping the table.

Thomas had gained weight since becoming the incumbent CEO at Mount Eliyah Ent. He'd been eating very well, with one of the top salaries paid to any music exec in the industry. It was going to be next to impossible to convince him to leave.

"What are you drinking?" he asked me.

I bit my bottom lip, feeling like an idiot. Thomas Dyer was still my boss. He had full authority to fire me for drinking alcohol during lunch. "Tequila?" I said. It came out as a question. Then I said, "You don't mind, do you?"

"No. Sundi, c'mon. One glass won't be an issue."

Mmph. What he didn't know was that I was on round two.

Thomas ordered a plain Coke with house-cured salmon and smoked bacon. I ordered a salad and piled on the croutons and candied walnuts—and I made sure not to get another refill of tequila. We were halfway through our meal when I asked the first of three questions that La'Renz had texted me. I had been peeking at my phone periodically to make sure I worded them right. While plucking a walnut off the top of my salad by hand and popping it in my mouth, I made question 1 of 3 sound casual.

"Have you ever thought of leaving Mount Eliyah Ent.?"

Thomas shook his head no instantly. "I wanna retire here."

"You don't wanna grow?" I asked. This was my own question.

"Sundi, we're working at the number one label in the world. I'm CEO here. There is no more growing to do."

"There's always room for growth. That's the crutch of capitalism. No growth equals bankruptcy."

"If there's room for growth, then I'm doing it with Mount Eliyah. I've never made this much money in my life. I'm making more than almost every top dog in this industry."

"I know. But you used the word *almost*. If Mount Eliyah is the number one label in the world, then you should have the number one salary in the world."

He stared at me as if I crossed a line. "That's not always how it works."

"True. But when you were an A&R at TMG, you *were* the highest paid A&R in music history."

This fact should have made him smile but it didn't.

He said, "But do you know that no one else knows that or cares about that? Anyway, in today's standards I was grossly overpaid."

"I would rather be overpaid than underpaid. Eliyah Golomb runs you ragged. I'm not around you 24-7 but I see how stressed you've been. You should be compensated for it."

He chuckled. "If I go in there demanding more money I'd be a fool. Eliyah would fire me."

"That says a lot about the man you work for. With La'Renz, you wouldn't even have had to ask."

"Maybe." He folded a piece of bacon in his mouth whole and chewed for a minute. "But with Eliyah, I don't have to worry about him prouncing around the office high on cocaine starting fights with people."

"La'Renz was funny sometimes, you have to admit."

"Yeah. But he was dangerous *most* times."

I nodded, not denying that. Then I asked question 2 of 3: "Thomas, are you happy though? At Mount Eliyah, are you happy?"

"I guess."

"You guess?"

"I'm content, I'll put it that way."

"One thing you can't deny is that out of all the drama we went through at Taylor Music Group, it was never a dull moment. I don't remember going a day without hearing you laugh."

He looked at me with concern. "Have you been talking to La'Renz?"

My heart skipped a beat. I had been putting on the persuasion too heavy. "Uh ... no. Have you?"

"As a matter of fact I have. Nearly his first day out of prison he tried to attack me. I had to fend him off with a letter opener. You know he's out of prison, right?"

"Yes, I heard."

"I'm surprised he hasn't tried to contact you. After he attacked me I read in a blog that he broke a bouncer's hand trying to get in a club. He hasn't changed, Sundi. I know we're sitting here talking about the good ol' days that weren't always so good but the reality is we'll never live those days again. We live in a better day now, with restraint and a lot more structure. I wouldn't trade this for what we had, if that's what you're asking me. Let's not pretend that La'Renz wasn't a maniac. Let's not pretend that he didn't choke a bootlegger nearly to death against the tire of his Range Rover, because me and you both sat in the backseat and watched him do it. Let's not pretend that he didn't toss his young wife from the terrace of an architectural monument in a foreign country because she had the smarts to leave him for the company we're blessed to be working at now. We can talk about the past, but let's not pretend that it wasn't anything but what it was—and that's complete chaos."

Question 3 of 3 was, *Would you ever consider working for La'Renz Taylor again?* But I didn't ask it because I had a good idea what the answer would be.

***

I stepped off the elevator onto the second floor, and for a moment I thought Thomas was coming out with me. Then I remembered his stop was up top. I had gotten so wrapped up in reminiscing about the past that it had sort of slipped my mind again that he was my boss here.

At Taylor Music Group, he had felt more like an equal.

"Thanks for lunch," I said to him with a smile, still putting on the charm. I was holding my clutch purse at my midsection. I turned slightly as if heading away from the elevators, but I really just wanted him to see the curve of my *bee-hind* before the doors closed. It felt wrong playing with an old friend's mind like this, but this is what La'Renz wanted me to do. "See you later, I guess."

Thomas tapped one of the buttons, keeping the door open longer. "We should schedule another lunch. I don't want to end on a 'see you later.' It's too open-ended. I like concrete times and dates."

"Okay. Promise not to be late next time?"

He smiled. "I promise."

"Well, you pick where we go and when. Email me or inbox me what you come up with."

"How 'bout I call you?"

"Even better."

I was asking myself what the hell did I just do, as I headed back to my work area. I had flirted with Thomas Dyer, and he seemed to actually believe I liked him beyond the realm of friendship. It made me feel sleazy, a feeling that didn't sit well in my heart—the exact same feeling I had resigned myself to over and over again when I was in an adulterous relationship with La'Renz in the past.

I promised myself I would go to church this Sunday and repent. Really actually go this time.

Closing my office door behind me, I slid my purse strap off my shoulder. And not until I turned on the lights did I notice that someone had been in here. I was for sure I'd had a visitor because my whole damn company computer was gone from my desk! I noticed that my packages, my faxes, my sticky notes, and even my external hard drive was missing too. But they left my power cables and adapters.

A bunch of cords, but all my stored information was *gone*. Everything had been intact before I left for lunch and I was for sure I had locked my door. I always locked it.

I stormed out of my office and went next door, walking in on my co-worker who rarely ever left the building for lunch.

"Did you see who went in my office?" I asked her accusingly, as if she had something to do with it.

She frowned without taking her eyes off of her computer, then finally glanced at me. "No, Sundi. Did you lock it?"

I shut her door without answering her dumb question, then went back in my room and felt a small rage quaking inside of me as I sat down on my empty desk and tried to figure this ordeal out.

Had I been fired? If so, why? Did Eliyah Golomb find out somehow that I was working for La'Renz again? Why didn't Thomas give me a heads-up?

Then, as if to answer my questions, my phone buzzed. I looked at it and saw that I had just received a work email from human resources. The preview

bar across my screen read "URGENT," and that made me afraid to open it up.

Heart beating fast, I tapped the bar with my thumb and began reading my fate.

From: MEENT Human Resources
To: Sundi Ashworth
Subject: Termination

Hello Ms. Ashworth,

Your employment at Mount Eliyah ENT (MEENT) will be terminated as of today. The workforce is changing and your position is no longer needed to fulfill this company's ongoing needs. Attached to this email you will find a detailed statement of your severance package in pdf format. If you have any questions or concerns about this correspondence or the attached file, please contact human resources during business hours (8am-4:30pm). Thank you.

Good Luck To You,

Natalie Mance
MEENT, HR Rep

CHAPTER 2

Kirbie Amor
Manhattan, New York

I had been recording with Timbuck, a Grammy-winning producer whom La'Renz had scheduled me to work with, for five hours straight now. My throat was stiflingly dry as I stepped away from the microphone and pulled my headphones off my head, resting them on my shoulders.

I needed a breather but I didn't want to quit.

"Take five," said Timbuck through his state-of-the-art pushbutton intercom system.

I glanced out the sound-proof glass at him, saw him waving for me to come on out the booth. He was a big guy with genuine muscle, more like a fitness trainer than a famous guy who made great music for a living. He was wearing a plain white tee that would've dwarfed my frame but looked appropriately small on him. From the waist down he wore even tighter designer joggers. Coras did that sometimes too, the small equals big thing, but Coras wasn't nearly as buff as Timbuck.

I showed the producer my forefinger, which meant "one more time." I wanted to get this song perfect and not look like an amateur who got tired easily.

"No, you need a break," he insisted. "Come out of there, Kirbie. I can tell when an artist is tapped."

I hung my headphones on its stand and left the booth. Timbuck had a chair for me and a bottled water already on hand.

"Tip your head back for me," he said to me after I sat.

"Do what?" I asked.

"Tip your head back and open your mouth. Trust me."

I did what he asked, feeling like a baby bird waiting on a worm. I watched him uncap the water and softly take hold of my chin as he poured the bottled water in my mouth with his other hand.

"That's it. Drink up. You should be feeling better already. Drink it, baby."

It filled my mouth slowly and I swallowed what I could, trying not to choke.

"More?" he asked me.

"Umm ..." I did want more but I'd rather not drink from his hand again so I said, "No, I'm fine. Thank you, Timbuck. I needed that."

He sat back down and scooted his chair so close to me our knees touched. "You have to let me know when you're feeling fatigued. You have a million-dollar voice and we don't wanna overwork it. You could do permanent damage."

"I just don't like starting and stopping a lot," I said. "I wanna get it done and done right."

This was a flat-out lie. I was the take-a-break queen back home at Gee Beats's studio. Coras was the one who always complained about me stopping and starting and not getting things done in a timely manner. But I wanted to impress Timbuck and ultimately La'Renz, who dropped me off here early this afternoon and told me specifically to *give it your all.*

"The only way it's gonna get done right is if we're enjoying ourselves," said the muscle-bound producer. "And we can't have fun if your throat is in knots."

"I agree."

"Let me loosen you up."

Timbuck hooked his fingertips behind my knees and, with little effort, pulled me closer to him until I was sitting on the edge of my chair and our knees were in between each other's legs. He brought his hands up to my neck and delicately massaged trigger points just under both ears. It felt amazing and heavenly, causing me to close my eyes and let his professional fingertips manipulate my tight skin.

"Breathe normal," he said. "Don't hold your breath."

"Sorry."

"Take it easy. Think fun and relaxation. Think of a sapphire blue ocean whistling against the wind."

I chuckled and so did he, as he flexed my neck sideways bringing one ear down closer to my shoulder. Tilting me to the other side, he said, "You know why La'Renz brought you here?"

"Mmm-hmm," I hummed melodically, my eyes still closed.

"Why?" he said, testing me.

"To make hits," I answered.

"Not just hits. But classics. Anybody can make a hit and be here today and gone tomorrow. But I only produce classics. Everlasting music. My first classic piece was with Caylene Hope over fifteen years ago. I also produced Jazzmine Short's

breakout single. That's why La'Renz brought you here. He knows I'm the best."

"I'm a fan of your work," I said.

"Are you?"

"Yes. But an even bigger fan of yours than me is a producer friend of mine named Gee Beats from my hometown. He's recovering from being shot still but you're like his idol and he won't believe I got a chance to work with you."

I could remember when Gee told me how he started out producing music. He would take tracks made by Timbuck and other super-producers and try to re-create them from scratch, by ear. From those beginnings, he crafted his own sound and became a real talent locally. I had heard of Gee through word-of-mouth before I met him. That's how good he got.

And now I was sitting here with one of his inspirations, enjoying an impressive neck massage.

How cool is this!

"You know one thing that's gonna give you an advantage over Jazzmine Short?" Timbuck said.

"What might that be?" I asked.

"Your natural beauty far exceeds hers."

I opened my eyes—and Timbuck was staring into me with an intense desire that seemed primal and ... threatening. This close I could see the age lines in his face, and it reminded me that he was closer in age to my father than myself. Also, with his hands lingering on my skin as he stared me down—*why was he still staring at me anyway?*—the danger-sensing part of my brain jolted me with memories of tabloids I'd read as a teen that I thought I had forgotten. In his heyday Timbuck had been rumored to sleep with a lot of female artists whose careers he'd help boost, including Jazzmine Short (before her marriage to La'Renz) and even Caylene Hope (though this rumor held little plausibility). Timbuck was a known music industry playboy and I had walked in here without even taking that into account.

I wanted him to let me go.

"Close your eyes again," he said to me softly. "I'm not finished."

"Um ... I'm loose now. Thank you." I put my hands on top of his, thinking he'd let me go. When he didn't, I moved my hands to his wrists. He still didn't budge. "I'm ready to get back in the booth, Tim. Thank you for the massage."

"I said close your eyes. I'm the professional here. I know what's best for you. I've done this a thousand times."

I bet you have.

"And I know *me*," I said with a smirk, trying to throw a playful spin on my sudden assertiveness. "I'm ready to sing."

"Close your eyes and take your hands off of my wrists. Let me finish, Kirbie. And then you sing." It sounded like a threat.

I had been in situations in the streets where I felt unsafe, but nothing compared to how I felt now. I had been robbed at gunpoint with a workboot crushing my face, I had sat in a restaurant blindfolded with a notorious Mexican Mafia boss and had more trust in him than I did in Timbuck. This wasn't right. And if Timbuck had been somebody I sold pills to, I would've already put him in his place.

But since that life was behind me, I closed my eyes and let my hands fall into my lap.

I heard Timbuck take a deep breath, then his strong fingertips plied into me again. It seemed to hurt this time, and I wasn't sure if he was pressing harder or if I was just annoyed.

"You got tense again," he said.

"I think you went past your mark. You might be overdoing it. You can stop."

"No, you just need more relief."

His cool minty breath against my neck alerted me that he'd leaned in close. My eyes popped open and I pulled away, but not before he planted a kiss on my jawline.

I stood up. "Nigga, I have a fiancé—!"

He stood up and, before I could finish my sentence, grabbed me by the face and forced another kiss on my mouth, mashing my lips painfully against my teeth. I tried to push him away but his huge arms were overwhelmingly solid and thick. The more I tried to pull away, the harder he squeezed my face together between his clawing hand. I literally thought he was going to crush every bone in my face one-handed.

Just when I realized I couldn't breathe, he broke the kiss. And I didn't think he did it for my sake; he probably hadn't been able to breathe either.

"Why are you fighting me?" he asked through heavy panting.

"Because I want you to get your fucking hands off of me!" I screamed at him. The real Kirbie had come out of me. I could give a damn about saving face for my career in this industry. This man was out of line, and I had hurt people for far less shit. "I'm not gonna tell you again, nigga!"

He grinned. "Or what?"

I struggled with him but he was just too damn strong. He ended up folding me backwards on his digital mixing interface. The knobs pressing into my back, all up and down my spine, felt like spikes.

"I'm not the person you wanna say no to," he hissed. "This industry is about give and take. You give ... and you take. I'm not getting paid for this session. La'Renz didn't give me a damn thing, and I don't do SHIT out of the kindness of my heart."

I wondered, *Is he implying that La'Renz expects me to spread my legs?*

"I'll pay you!" I blurted. One of his large hands covered my whole jaw from side to side. The fleshy meat between his thumb and forefinger sat on my bottom lip. I was tempted to bite but didn't.

"You think you can afford me? La'Renz can't afford me but you think you can?"

"I'm not broke. I really have the cash. I can wire it to you. I was a hustler way before I took singing seriously. I don't want a hand-out from you. I'll pay my own way."

"So now you want me to believe that the pills and drug-dealing you sing about is fact?"

"It is!"

He laughed. "Y'know, Jazzmine Short didn't put up nearly as much fight as you. And that's because she knew the importance of give and take. Producers run this industry now. You *need* me. I don't need you—or your money, even if I did believe you had it. I want this pussy."

"No!"

He screamed back at me mockingly. "No!"

"I swear to God, nigga! If you don't stop ...!"

"I swear to God, nigga," he parroted, as his free hand went under my shirt. He chuckled. "You're gonna thank me for this. After it's all said and done you're gonna be topping the charts, and then you're gonna come back to me begging to suck my dick for another hit song."

He nodded at me suddenly, as if he was agreeing with himself. I thought he was crazy—or crazier!—until he turned his head and I saw blood in his hair. Then I watched La'Renz swing another fist that caught Timbuck off guard again. The hulking producer released me to defend himself against my boss.

"What was you tryna do to my artist, muthafucka?!" La'Renz roared. He was unbuttoning his cuffs, rolling the sleeves up on his athletic-cut Prada dress shirt. He loosened his tie and snatched it off. "Try doing that to me!"

Timbuck touched the back of his head, caressing the blood there that was caused by La'Renz's diamond pinky ring. I thought the madness was over, but Timbuck shocked me and apparently La'Renz too when he charged at La'Renz like a linebacker. The booming *thud* I heard when Timbuck slammed into La'Renz must have knocked the wind out of him.

They hit the ground, Timbuck on top.

But La'Renz had enough remaining strength or adrenaline to grapple with the producer's arms, managing to lock onto his head, trying to snap it off it seemed like. But Timbuck's head was too big, his neck a tree trunk. I feared if Timbuck straddled La'Renz, as he was clearly trying to do, then the fight would get ugly. So I stepped in, just like I would have done for Archie or my dad ... or Coras.

I ghetto-stomped on the back of Timbuck's head, then flopped on his back and wrapped my arms around his big-ass neck. He rolled over and I ended up under him. I nearly suffocated, but La'Renz was right there again to save me. The three of us were fighting on the floor for what seemed like hours but could have only been minutes—or even seconds. I sustained a brutal elbow to my forehead but got my legs locked around one of

Timbuck's arms, allowing La'Renz to pound him almost without any repercussion. When Timbuck finally got free, he scrambled across the floor on all fours, to the other side of the room. He rested against the acoustic foam on the far wall.

I pulled myself up on a chair.

La'Renz stood up and flicked open a pocket knife.

"I'm done," Timbuck moaned.

"Says who?" La'Renz closed half of the distance between them. "I ain't seen enough blood yet."

"La'Renz, chill. I'm done. Yall win."

"I'm still wondering what the fuck you were trying to do to my artist."

"Nothing." Timbuck was heaving, his breath not coming fast enough. "We just had a misunderstanding."

"Really?!" I shrieked. "A misunderstanding? You tried to rape me!"

"Just get out of here," Timbuck said, waving us off, "and let's act like nothing happened here. Just go."

"We're not going nowhere until you produce her a hit," La'Renz said adamantly.

Timbuck stared at La'Renz in disbelief. And so did I. I wanted to get out of here just as bad as Timbuck wanted us to.

"Get'cho big-ass up and sit down at your mixer and start mixing!" La'Renz ordered, pointing with his knife. "Kirbie, get back in that goddamn booth and sing."

None of us moved for a moment, then Timbuck slowly got to his feet and eventually seated in his chair; it squeaked under his weight, a sound that broke the heavy silence among us. He peeked over his shoulder at La'Renz as if still wondering if he had to go through with this. La'Renz fixed me with a look and pointed with his knife for me to get moving also. Reluctantly, I waltzed in the booth and put the headphones on.

I would've never imagined that we'd turn out a hit song after that fight, but we did. Timbuck even smiled at me a few times and gave me a couple thumbs-ups through the soundproof glass when I was recording my ad-libs. I actually felt real confident about what we were creating.

After the session, after I was out of the booth and putting on my jacket, La'Renz sort of forced me and Timbuck to pose for a quick picture. He

told Timbuck to edit out any noticeable bruises and cuts and post it on his Site page.
    I didn't think he'd do it.
    But I was wrong.

TimbuckGrammyGangsta posted a photo

TimbuckGrammyGangsta: Had a BANGING session with newcomer Kirbie Amor! Yall won't believe what we just put down. She's the real deal! And I cosign that! Wait till yall hear what we crafted! Classic shit!—*with* **Kirbie Amor.**

CHAPTER 3

Sammy "Hitman" Russtrip
Manhattan, New York

Me and my son were eating dinner at a tiny diner across the street from Timbuck's studio, waiting on La'Renz and his artist to come back out. An hour ago we watched him run in to get her.

I didn't know how much longer they'd be so I ordered another coffee. Dark roast, three sugars, three creamers. Here, they made you add the extras yourself, which I preferred.

My son was sitting across from me. He was on his phone, again.

"If they walked out of that studio right now, you wouldn't even notice," I said to him.

Jarvis looked out the window, past our silver Yukon. When he didn't see our little birds, he went back to his phone. "I'm paying attention. But you're the lookout, I'm the researcher," he told me.

"Since when did you get the authority to assign job titles?"

"Look at this, daddy." He showed me his phone.

"I told you to call me Sammy on-duty. Might as well call me Sammy off-duty too to minimize mistake."

"Sammy, look."

I looked at his phone and saw a picture of our target's young recruit, Kirbie Amor, smiling with super-producer Timbuck. "Okay, whoopty-do. Why is this relevant?"

"This picture was posted to The Site a few minutes ago."

"And?"

"*And* you keep complaining about me being on my phone but I'm doing us both a favor by keeping eyes on our birds. Digitally."

"La'Renz isn't in the picture. He's our target, not her."

"But wherever she is, he's never too far away. The Site helps us locate 'em. It's easier than following them everywhere they go every day."

"Easier is not always better."

"In who's book?"

I pounded my fist on the table, not that loud but hard enough to rattle the cutlery. "We are not gonna rely on your phone to tell us where they are. We practice old-fashioned, tried-and-true investigating. You have to have eyes on who you plan to murder."

"We're wasting time. It's getting boring. We could be sitting at home or with some bitches, following La'Renz's moves through social media. When Eliyah gives the word, then we can go hard on the investigating."

"It'll be too late then. When Eliyah calls, we already have to be in place. And social media wouldn't have told us that La'Renz is staying with Sundi Ashworth. Did he post that?"

Jarvis scratched his head. "No. But I'm just saying ... my phone helps."

"Your phone is making you lazy."

"You're set in your ways, daddy—uh, Sammy."

"I am. And you need to be set in my ways too if you plan to survive in this field. Pulling the trigger is the easy part. It's what you do before and after that counts. Did your phone just alert you that our birds are leaving the building?"

He turned and saw La'Renz and his female singer across the street climbing into the back of

a non-descript Lincoln Town Car. This Lincoln, I knew, was a hired driver from a Manhattan company with a fleet of cars used to chauffeur the rich around the city clandestinely.

Jarvis shot out of his seat, heading for the door.

I caught up with him quick and grabbed his shoulder from behind. "Forgetting something?" I said.

He looked back to where we were sitting and saw his coat laying in the booth seat. He went to grab it, and when he came back I stopped him again.

"Forgetting something else?"

"What?" he said, irritated.

"I guess you want us on the news for a dine-and-dash, huh?"

"Oh shit. My bad, Sammy."

He dropped two twenties on the table, overpaying by at least fifteen bucks.

"Now get the door for me," I said, shoving him ahead of me. "Hurry up, knucklehead."

I was on his ass.

CHAPTER 4

La'Renz "Buddy Rough" Taylor
Brooklyn Heights

I poured Kirbie a glass of Bacardi. "I'm so sorry about that. Fuck, if I would've known that nigga Timbuck was a creep I would've took you to another producer. He's not the only hotshot in town."

"There's no way you could have known he'd do that," Kirbie said, as she took a sip of the liquor. She set the glass down on one of Sundi's *Long Live Happy Hour* coasters, keeping the moisture off of the cherry veneer tabletop. She had been respectful of Sundi's home, in every way, since she got here. This little girl had manners. She added, "Nobody would've saw that coming. Timbuck just came out of nowhere with that shit."

"I'm sorry."

"Don't apologize. It's not your fault."

But it *was* my fault. I knew Timbuck would try to work his way in between Kirbie's legs. Sleeping with young talent—it was what he did, what he thrived off of. It was an industry hush thing that, if you didn't want to pay Timbuck's exorbitant studio fees, then just send him ripe potential in the form of the opposite sex. I didn't think Kirbie would say no. How many 19-year-olds would turn down an athletic, multi-millionaire music icon? However, the last thing I expected was for Timbuck to try and *take it from her* ...

Kirbie was supposed to fuck him willingly.

Just like Jazzmine had.

"Do you think he's gonna tell people what happened?" Kirbie asked.

"No. It would work against him if he did that. Who would broadcast to the world that you got your ass beat? He's probably more worried about *us* telling the tabloids what went down." I gave Kirbie a look that said, *You're not gonna report this, right?*

"Nobody has to worry about me saying anything. I don't want my career to start off with a scandal."

"Exactly. Because that's just the type of publicity that our enemies would use against us. I'm sure Eliyah would have his PR attack dogs feed more bullshit into the story. He'd find a way to turn it around and say me and you are liable, we're the criminals. He's done it before."

Kirbie looked hesitant, and I wasn't sure why.

"What is it?" I pressed. "Did you already tell somebody what happened?"

"No ... umm ... I got a friend request from Eliyah Golomb on The Site."

"You didn't accept it, did you?"

"... Yes."

"Dammit!" I stood up fast, putting my hands on my hips. I glared at her. "Do you know what you just did? Now he thinks he has a chance of stealing you from me."

"That's not gonna happen. I'm a loyal person. I accepted it because ... it was just social media. Caylene Hope friended me too. They both did, right after our radio interview at Revolt."

"Eliyah is the enemy. You were wrong for that, Kirbie. Common sense should've told you to ignore him."

"I can unfriend him."

Sighing, I said, "No. Then he'll know I told you to do it and he'll really know he got to me." I sighed again. "We're gonna keep it like it is. Maybe he'll think I authorized you accepting his friend request.

But from here on out, if it has anything to do with Eliyah Golomb you let me know, before you make any sudden decisions. Is that clear?"

She nodded. "Yes. Crystal clear."

***

When I saw Sundi pull her Volvo truck in the driveway earlier than normal, I got even more anxious about knowing how her day went. She was supposed to have had lunch with Thomas Dyer and planted the seed of unrest and dissatisfaction in his head.

I held the front door open when she walked up.

"Hi, honey," I smiled, exaggerating the politeness. It felt good answering the door for a beautiful lady and not a correctional officer. "How was your day?"

She didn't smile back. Her hair was all in her face in strands of distress. And when I tried to help her out of her coat, she nearly shrugged it off onto the floor. I caught it and hung it up and then followed her into the kitchen, where she grabbed the bottle of Bacardi that me and Kirbie had been drinking on a couple hours ago.

Sundi poured the alcohol into a large wine glass. I was worried because she hadn't said a thing to me yet.

"It didn't go as planned?" I asked.

"Fuck no." She tucked some of her hair behind her ear and I noticed that she'd been crying. Then she covered her face with the see-through wine glass for a whole half minute as she gulped down the liquor. "I got fired," she announced.

My heart started beating fast. I already knew what this meant. "Eliyah knows you're working for me."

She shook her head no. "That's what I thought at first. But I got fired because the A&R position has been less and less needed over the years. With the internet, you don't have to go out and find talent anymore. To be honest, for the last year or so I thought Eliyah was keeping me around just so I'd have a job."

"That's not why you got fired. He knows, Sundi. The muthafucka knows!"

"How would he know we're working together? We're always covering our tracks and we barely ever go out in public together. Plus, I talked to Thomas

after I found out I was terminated and he looked into it immediately. He told me the A&R position is being replaced by a computerized algorithm that searches the internet for substantial Likes and video hits on its own. A robot took my position."

"Thomas lied to you," I said.

"Thomas has never lied to me in his life. He's still the same Thomas we both used to know."

"What did he say when you asked him if he'd ever work for me again?"

She paused, blinking twice. "He said he wasn't sure. It was something he'd have to think about."

I leaned against the counter and crossed my arms. For some reason I didn't think Thomas said that. "Eliyah knows you're on my team. I know he knows. I can feel it. He has someone watching us, someone following us."

"How do you know that?" she asked, still unbelieving.

"Because I used to have watchers."

In my glory days, I learned that in order to stay ahead of the game you had to have inside knowledge on your competition. I had people—spies, really—who would report to me on a weekly and sometimes daily basis, informing me of new musical acts and other labels' secret marketing strategies.

I even had one spy who would break the law for me.

Even murder for me.

His name was Sammy "Hitman" Russtrip. I wondered what he was up to ...

"That doesn't mean Eliyah has watchers too," Sundi said.

"Why wouldn't he?"

Before she could reply, I went to the kitchen window blinds and pulled a few plastic slats down to peek outside. The first car I saw that rubbed me wrong was parked against the curb, idling. It was a silver Yukon Denali with tinted windows.

"Where are you going?" Sundi asked as I stormed out the kitchen.

I went outside and started walking fast toward the idling Yukon. I put my hands in my slacks pockets, pretending I was on a casual stroll, as my right hand fingered my pocket knife. As soon as I stepped onto the pavement of Willow Street about to cross to the idling Yukon, I heard the huge SUV shift into gear.

Craaank.

I halted, then watched it *vroom* forward and off down the street.

There was no doubt in my mind now. *He's watching me.*

He's tracking me.

"What the hell were you about to do to that car?" Sundi asked me when I came back in the house.

I closed the front door and locked it. "Whatever would've needed to be done."

"La'Renz, you're paranoid!"

"Think so? Well why did that car take off like that?"

"Like what? It just pulled off and left like any other vehicle in the world does."

"No. Whoever was in that Yukon was watching us. How many Yukon Denalis with tinted windows do you know that idle in Brooklyn Heights?"

"Cars idle all the time in this neighborhood."

"Bullshit. Eliyah is on to us. That's why you were fired. Thomas is in on it too. That muthafucking traitor."

"Thomas is still one of us, at heart. I know it. He said he was gonna work on getting my job back. He's gonna call me within a week."

"That call is never gonna come. You're still naive, Sundi. People you grow with change all the time. They betray you and disappoint you. It's a part of life."

Suddenly, Sundi's phone went off. We both heard it ringing in her purse. She grabbed it, then gave me a "told you so" wink before answering it.

"Hello?" she asked while staring at me.

I could tell by her eyes that she was talking to Thomas Dyer. And when she smiled, for some reason my heartrate started picking up. Good news, maybe?

Thomas is coming to work for me again, I thought with hope.

Sundi covered the mouth of her phone with her hand, then whispered to me, "Thomas said Eliyah wants to have a meeting with me, in person at his mansion."

I wasn't expecting that. "About what?" I asked, skeptical.

"About getting my job back," she said as if it were obvious. "What do you want me to tell Thomas? Should I go?"

My gut-feeling said no. But if there was any chance to pull wool over Eliyah's eyes, then this could be it. Sundi could convince him that she wasn't working for me; I knew that was what this meeting was about. Eliyah was like me in that sense—he'd

want to stare his enemy in the face and make her confess.

Sundi just had to be careful.

"Tell him you're going," I decided.

CHAPTER 5

Sundi Ashworth
Brooklyn, New York

I lifted the metal hinge on the large oak door of Eliyah Golomb's mid-1800s brownstone and used it to knock three times; it reverberated inside—*boom, boom, boom.* A moment later the door opened.

"Who are you?" said an elderly Latina in an Adidas tracksuit that fit loose and wrinkly on her thin frame. "Are you lost?"

"No, I'm at the right place. My name's Sundi Ashworth and I'm here to see Mr. Eliyah Golomb," I said. "He told me to meet him here. I work for him."

Well, I used to work for him.

The old woman inspected me with her dark eyes, as if she'd heard bad things about me. I didn't know if she was a maid, the host, or some other type of help. I had ruled out kinship because of

her deep Spanish accent. "Come in, Ms. Ashworth. He's expecting you."

She led me into the mansion at a pace that was surprisingly hard to keep up with—it was annoying listening to her fleece track pants *swish* together as she walked ahead of me so I was glad when we reached the sunlit parlor; it had flawless cream carpeting and large windows. I was a little nervous stepping onto the carpet, not sure if the soles of my Giuseppe heels had tracked in dirt, so I took them off before I had a seat. I set them in my lap.

The maid—or whoever she was—looked at me judgingly, and it made me think my skirt was too short or I didn't have approval to remove my shoes. Then she brought a walkie-talkie to her lips and clicked the talk button. The device chirped.

"Come in, Eliyah."

A short pause, then Eliyah's stately voice came through: "Yes, Rose?"

"Ms. Ashworth is here." She said my name with bitterness. "Do you want me to send her up or make her wait? Over."

"I'll be down in just a sec."

"Copy. Should I keep an eye on her? Over."

"No, Rose. Please finish attending to your duties. She's fine. She won't steal anything." Eliyah chuckled, but it came out as heavy radio static.

"10-4. Over and out." Rose turned it off, then fixed me with a glare. Crow's feet pinched the corners of her eyes. "Make yourself at home, Ms. Ashworth. Mr. Golomb will be with you shortly."

Like I didn't just hear him say that ...

Immediately after Rose left me alone I had a sudden foreboding feeling of guilt. It was the same feeling I used to get in middle school when I had to wait my turn to see the principal. I had always managed to talk my way out of after-school detention, but I was less confident here in this mansion as I mentally prepared to convince Eliyah to give me my job back.

Then I received a timely text from La'Renz.

> **La'Renz Taylor:** Don't let him intimidate you. Eliyah is a weak man that tries to come across as a threat. Remind him that he needs you, not the other way around.

I quickly sent him a text back that said *I'll call you when I leave*, then I silenced my phone so there'd be no interruptions when Eliyah finally came down to talk to me.

I looked around the parlor admiringly and then outward, beyond the second wood-burning fireplace where all of this lavish architecture formed a V in the center of the home. Past that, this 5-story mansion split into two hallways that led to other luxurious corners—like a grand formal dining room and upstairs to more posh rooms you could get lost in.

And I wasn't just guessing about the rooms. I had been all over this mansion years ago. It used to belong to La'Renz. But Eliyah bought it at a foreclosure auction after La'Renz went to prison.

"And there she is."

Eliyah caught me by surprise. I turned and looked up. I had been so busy looking forward that I had forgotten there was a balcony above me. How long had Eliyah been watching me? Was he able to read the text La'Renz sent me from there?

I stood up. "How are you, sir?"

"Don't call me sir, Sundi. We have history."

"Well what am I supposed to call you? I can't call you boss anymore."

I got right to it like La'Renz had wanted me to. No beating around the bush. And it seemed as if Eliyah wasn't ready for my frank approach. His face went bland; he was just holding the railing and staring at me like he had expected me to come here and be happy that I was even invited.

I'm not a fawning type of girl, and you know that, Mr. Golomb.

Eliyah was a boldly handsome man. His suit was finely tailored, fitting his lithe frame perfectly. His hair was short, thick and blonde, and looked brushed through with gel—a rather casual look for a multi-millionaire, but it made him seem humble (except that I knew otherwise). In an issue of *Music Swag Weekly* he was voted Man of the Year, which was the first title given to a man of Jewish decent since the urban magazine started commending industry achievements.

"Do you remember where the conference room is?" he asked me, his tone professional now.

"I do," I answered.

"I'll meet you there."

When I got to the conference room he was already sitting—but he was seated on *top* of the table and swinging his legs like a kid.

"Where do I sit?" I asked.

He patted the hand-carved wood next to him. "Right here. Right next to me."

"This is an informal meeting?"

"I never said this was a meeting at all."

I set my purse and shoes in a chair, then scooched my butt on top of the table with him. It felt almost natural to start swinging my legs too but I didn't because he'd probably get the idea that

I was here as an old friend—two buddies at the pier chatting it up with our feet in the water—but I wasn't. I was a fired employee who was here to figure out why.

"You look agitated," he said.

"I am."

"Why? Because I let you go?"

I stared at him tight-lipped, trying to keep from cursing. I replied in a polite voice, "Yes, because you fired me, Eliyah."

"Well how did you think I felt when I found out you're working for La'Renz Taylor?"

I hesitated, but not long. "I'm not working for La'Renz Taylor," I said straight-faced.

"My sources tell me otherwise."

"What sources?"

"They've seen you together."

"You have people watching me?" I said indignantly.

"No. I have people watching *La'Renz*. And you happened to be in close proximity to him. Very close proximity."

La'Renz was right! I screamed in my head. And I didn't know where to go from here. I didn't know how much evidence he had.

"I had to fire you, Sundi. It's a conflict of interest. And even more than that I'm hurt to my heart that you would throw away the opportunity I gave you. I took you in when no one else would."

"I'm not working for him. I'm just ... helping him out."

"In what way?"

"He just got out of prison. He has nothing, no money."

"La'Renz still has millionaire friends in this industry that owes him. I've heard he's been collecting money since he got out. If he told you he didn't have money then he lied to you. Is he living with you?"

I was certain that Eliyah already knew the answer to this question.

"Temporarily," I said.

"I hate to hear that. You moved a crackhead into your home. And you promised me you would never go back to him."

I remembered that promise. I uttered it when me and Eliyah were well into our relationship, long after La'Renz had been sent to prison. Eliyah and I dated for almost two years and managed to keep our relationship out of the media's eye. It was soon after he hired me when we started dating, and not until after a year and a half of courting did I give myself to him sexually.

That's when things went downhill. It got to a point where I felt like all I did was put his penis in my mouth on-call; he was too tired or too busy to lay with me. It started to feel like a job. Then I started seeing in him qualities I'd hated in La'Renz—like the fact that he thought he owned me. Sometimes I even thought Eliyah was deliberately trying to act like La'Renz, either because that's what he thought I wanted or because that's who he was turning into.

We managed to break it off cordially and he never fired me. Until now.

I looked at him hard and said adamantly, "I'm not with La'Renz."

"Okay. Did you tell him that we used to talk?" Eliyah inquired.

You must think I'm crazy. He'd kill me if he found that out.

"It's none of his business," I said.

"I don't want to see you go down the same path as before. He's gonna pull you down with him this time. You're better than that. You have so much to lose."

"Like my job, for instance?"

He sighed. "Do you want your job back?"

"Yes."

"Then get rid of La'Renz. The day you get him out of your house is the day you're re-hired. But I can't have you working for me, with him in your home. He'll be a bad influence on you, which would ultimately affect my company."

There had to be some rule or law against firing somebody because of what they did in their personal life, but I'd be naive to think this type of treatment didn't happen to people all the time. I looked over at my purse, wanting to call La'Renz and tell him that we didn't need me working inside Mount Eliyah ... but I knew that wasn't true, that I was just tired of sitting here kissing his ass. In all actuality I could really get a lot of industry info from the inside that could really help Taylor Music Group stay ahead of the curve.

Eliyah's hand suddenly grabbed my chin and jerked it back toward him so he could look me in the eyes.

"Are you sleeping with him again?" he asked firmly.

"No," I lied.

"Sundi, where did we go wrong?"

"I don't think anything went wrong. Our relationship just ran its course."

"I know I mistreated you a little bit, but I know it wasn't anything as bad as La'Renz."

"Eliyah, I need to go. I have some thinking to do."

"Do you hate me?"

"I'm not in the hate business."

"I still love you."

This made me angry. I felt like Eliyah was only trying to win me back because La'Renz was in my life again. I started to question if Eliyah had ever cared about me at all, or if I was just another notch under his belt.

"I have to go," I told him.

Eliyah's hand tried to find its way around my waist as I hopped down off the table. But it fell away as I distanced myself to grab my purse and heels. His needy fingertips just barely grazed my backside, and I hated to admit that it was actually a nice sensation.

Pulling my purse strap on my shoulder, I headed for the nearest exit.

"Sundi," he called.

I turned. "Yes, Eliyah?"

"Get that crackhead out of your house," he said with a familiar selfishness, then pushed down off the table (it was a *push* and not a *hop* because he was a lot taller than me). He reached in his pocket where he found his cigar and lighter. He lit up, and I thought he was about to walk toward me with the smoke but instead he paused in front of his floor-to-ceiling wall of art that pictorialized the military and political leader Napoléon Bonaparte in exile on the island of Saint Helena.

He seemed disappointed with the artistic scene before him, as if the French emperor had let him down.

Then Eliyah turned to me and added, "Because bad things don't just happen to bad people. They happen to the good people who are around them just the same."

CHAPTER 6

Sundi Ashworth
Brooklyn Heights

"That's not a problem. I'll leave."
"You're gonna give in?"
"It's not giving in, Sundi."
I actually expected La'Renz to say no. He was letting Eliyah dictate where he could and couldn't live and I was just baffled that he was being so nonchalant about it.

It sort of offended me too. *Is he tired of living with me already?*

"We can be more discreet," I suggested. "You don't have to leave. You can just go out the back whenever we have to go somewhere."

"That won't make a difference. Whoever Eliyah has watching me will know I'm still living here and he won't give you your job back."

"He *has* to give me my job back. He can't fire me because I have you living with me. I can sue him."

La'Renz let out a crude laugh. "Good luck with that."

He took his button-up shirt off in front of me, then folded it up into a neat, even tuck and set it on a pile with his other dirty clothes that I'd wash for him later. I had told him that he didn't need to fold the dirties, but I assumed he kept doing it because it was one of his lingering prison habits.

He left the room and walked across to the bathroom, where he cut on the shower. When he came back to finish undressing—in which he folded his slacks and undergarments as neatly as his shirt—he continued to make fun of my comment about suing Eliyah, predicting that I'd be lucky to leave the courtroom still owning my own vagina.

I didn't like being belittled, and I nearly made a remark about Eliyah owning my pussy in the past, but I swallowed the words hard. I silently watched him wrap a bath towel around his waist to cover his privates as he went back to the bathroom; he'd just started using the towel when Kirbie moved in, and even that took some convincing.

I wasn't done speaking with La'Renz yet.

So I undressed and joined him in the shower.

"When are you leaving?" I asked, washing his muscular back with a sponge full of soap suds.

"Tonight," he said.

I nearly dropped the sponge. After a pause to stabilize my anger, I continued to rub and wash. "Why so soon?"

"It'll look good on your part. He'll think you kicked me out immediately and he'll be less likely to think we're still working together. If we wait, he'll think we're coming up with a plan."

"Do we even have a plan after this?"

"Oh yeah we do."

"Care to share?"

"We get Kirbie acquainted with these new and established artists down south, where Eliyah has less influence."

"I know some people."

"And I'm gonna need your connections."

I squeezed the sponge over his head and let the suds snake down the dips and valleys of his back muscles. "So what hotel are you going to tonight? The same one across from Mount Eliyah ENT?"

"Yes, for tonight."

"And then what? You can't have your new artist living with you in a hotel. Kirbie will start to ask questions. She won't stick around. I can tell she's not the type of young girl you should bullshit around with."

"That's why I'm moving into a mansion in Atlanta."

I was pissed. I smacked him on the back, right there on his shoulder's anterior. With the wetness and the red mark it left, I know it stung. He spun around with the look of the devil. But I wasn't intimidated.

"The fuck you are!" I flared. "You're not leaving me here with Eliyah while you move out of town!"

"Why not?"

"Because I just got you back!"

"Sundi, we've done long distance before."

"But you were married then. We had to."

"We have to *now*. This is what the circumstances call for."

I held back tears. "So you're gonna buy a fucking mansion in Georgia? Why are you throwing away money like that? You could be putting that money into your artist."

"I leased the mansion."

"You already leased the—?" I couldn't even finish my sentence I was so infuriated. I bumped my bare chest against his, burying my nipples. "This isn't something you just decided to do. You already had this in place way before Eliyah fired me. You probably had this Atlanta move planned before you got out of prison. When were you gonna tell me?"

"I told you when I first got out that I wouldn't be staying with you long."

"But I thought you liked it here."

"I do. And I'd stay if Eliyah didn't know I was here. But he does. This move is necessary. I'm thinking long-term. I'm using my extrasensory perception."

"Using what?"

He turned back around, dipping his head under the stream of water from the showerhead nozzle, rinsing. If he thought the water would drown me out, he was wrong.

I screamed in his ear, "Am I in your long-term plan, nigga! Or am I just check one on your fucking prison release bucket list!"

He ignored me.

So I yelled louder. "LA'RENZ TAYLOR, you better ANSWER ME MUTHAFUCKER!"

Not until I grabbed his balls from behind did I get his attention—but not in the way I had expected.

He turned and grabbed me by the throat with lightning speed. Before I knew it the glass shower door shattered as he shoved me through it (I think accidentally). Slipping, I fell out onto the toilet and then hugged the lid to keep from falling all the way onto the floor with all the glass. Amazingly I wasn't bleeding or hurt. La'Renz stepped out of the shower and stood over me as if he were about to kill me.

"Rule number one," he growled. "Don't *ever* grab my dick while I'm in the shower unless I tell you to."

I felt like *I* was in prison now.

"Rule number two—you don't ever question what the fuck I do. I KNOW WHAT THE FUCK I'M DOING! And not you, Eliyah, or any of these other muthafuckas out here who got an opinion about La'Renz 'Buddy Rough' Taylor can tell me how to do this shit. I know how to win! I taught muthafuckas how to win! All you can do for me is fall in line. If not, then get the fuck on. Because I won't let my feelings for you get in the way this time. Not this time."

I knew how to deal with the Buddy Rough side of La'Renz. Just shut up and be quiet, let him blow his steam off. Don't antagonize.

Behind him, the showerhead continued to blast hot pressured water. And without a door it was

spraying over the waterproof pan onto the floor. Puddles were already starting to form on my tile.

"Can you cut the water off, please?" I asked him nicely.

CHAPTER 7

Kirbie Amor
Hunts Point, Bronx

I was dropped off at another studio in Hunts Point, an industrial neighborhood of the Bronx overran with train tracks and failed properties. La'Renz led me inside a graffiti-tagged building and up a flight of weak, unsteady steps with no hand rail. After a minute or so of walking I realized La'Renz didn't know where he was going, or at least it seemed that way by the constant craning of his neck around corners. But then a young Asian man with wireless headphones draped over his shoulders stuck his head out of a room and waved us over and I knew this was our producer.

He introduced himself as DJ East and shook both of our hands excitedly. He had a dimpled smile and scruffy hair. It seemed as though La'Renz had just met this guy or barely knew him, and I didn't feel comfortable being left alone with him, especially after what happened between me and Timbuck. But I had been in more bad-vibe situations than this—*way* more—when I sold pills with Archie, so I would have to deal with my discomfort like a lady, just like I'd done in the past.

About ten minutes into the session, after DJ East had let us listen to intros of several of his latest projects, my inner alarm system started to reach a calm. The music was growing on me. And I found myself tossing song themes around in my mind and mumbling lyrics that seemed to fit with the mood of the instruments.

I must have looked like I felt safe because that's when La'Renz pulled me to the side and told me he was leaving.

"I have to go but I want to make sure you're okay first," he said with his arm curled around my shoulder. He was starting to feel like a big brother. "Will you be okay?"

I nodded. "I'm fine. I like his beats."

"Cool."

Then La'Renz handed me a small .22 Ruger with a three-inch barrel—*a gun I didn't even know he had been carrying!*—and made me tuck it in the rear of my pants without DJ East seeing.

La'Renz lowered his voice even more. "If he gives you problems, shoot him. If you can make it out of here without putting a bullet in him, then do that. Because I don't know this nigga. I just met him in a club right after I got out of prison. But he's popular in the nightlife here and I want to get you established with a couple more DJs before we move south."

South. The word held so much weight with me. I was just starting to get familiar with the Big Apple and now we were packing up and going to Atlanta. La'Renz had just told me the news last night and I hadn't had a chance to tell Coras yet.

Or Archie, for that matter.

"Don't be afraid to use it," La'Renz went on. "There's a hammer on the top of it, this rounded spur thing at the back. Just click it down, aim and—"

"I know how to shoot," I said, cutting him off. It was times like this that I wished La'Renz knew me like some of my friends back home. Because he would have known that I was no stranger to revolvers or automatic pistols and assault rifles. The only weapon I had little experience with was a shotgun because they were big and short-ranged.

I figured that La'Renz must have had me stereotyped as this helpless little Kansas City girl, just

like those guys at Revolt had. La'Renz probably thought my lyrics were fake too.

Hmph. No big deal.

Over time, he'd learn.

"Next time bring me a .380," I whispered. "That's what I used to carry."

He smiled at me like I was lying, and then he patted me on the back and left.

Me and DJ East recorded three unbelievably great songs. My phone had been buzzing the whole time but I ignored it. I was shooting for a fourth song, trying to impress La'Renz with my work ethic, but DJ East intercommed me and told me to come out of the booth.

"Let's take a break," he said. "I can tell you're tired as hell."

This was the same thing Timbuck said to me, I thought.

I sat down near DJ East but far enough away to have time to react if he came at me. But for some reason I didn't think he would. He seemed more nervous than me.

"Kirbie, I couldn't wait to meet you," he said with an excited tremor in his voice. "I love how you do what you do."

"Thank you."

"Your lyrics sound real. Never heard nothing like it. Normally all girls sing about is love. You sing about selling pills."

I smiled politely. "Thanks. I write from experience."

"It'd be nice to get Coras on a track with you too."

My heart started beating fast, and I immediately got protective. "How the fuck do you know Coras?"

DJ East looked offended. "Who doesn't know Coras? He's a very popular underground artist here in New York. I play his music in the club every night and the crowd loves it. And throughout the night, if the dancers ever start to lull, I'll re-play one of you guys' songs together to get 'em hype again."

"Really?"

"Yes. Every night, literally. That's how I met La'Renz. I played one of your songs one night and he rushed up to me at the DJ booth trying to figure out who you were."

I was about to ask questions about La'Renz in connection to my music—because I was still confused about how he'd found my information—but my phone rang again. It was Archie. I wasn't

surprised. He'd been calling me nonstop the past few days.

I excused myself from DJ East and stood in the corner of the room and answered my cell. "Hello?"

"Harder to get in touch with than the president," Archie said bitterly.

"I'm working. I'm in the studio right now so I can't talk long."

"Don't have time for your fiancé?"

"I do. Just not a lot. How are you?"

"I saw you and Coras on The Site commenting back and forth under that picture with you and Timbuck. Do you think that's appropriate behavior for a female engaged to someone else?"

"Archie, I was corresponding with a lot of other fans too."

"Coras isn't a fan."

"Neither is Gee Beats and he was commenting too. Is Gee a problem also?"

"Just Coras. You know I don't like that bitch ass nigga. He's tryna fuck you. You may not see it, but I know how niggas think. And he's starting to comment on your posts more and more to make people think yall got something going on."

"Archie, if you called to talk about The Site then we should schedule this another time. I'm on the clock. I don't want to spend La'Renz's studio money on the phone."

"Speaking of money ..." Archie began, then he went quiet on me. A second later I heard a tiny buzzing sound similar to a hummingbird. His voice came back on: "Did you hear that?"

"Yeah, what was it?"

"That was the sound of me flipping through a hundred thousand dollars. Business is booming, Kirbie! You can quit that music shit and come on home to what you're good at."

I almost cursed at him. For Archie to imply that I was only good at selling drugs and not singing really hurt coming from him. But that reinforced my determination to make this first mixtape as good as it could be. Because if I didn't, I would have to go back home and peddle cocaine—or whatever drug was currently in demand—with Archie for the rest of my life. I wanted something better for us.

I told Archie I had to go and that I loved him, then I sat back down with DJ East.

"Sorry about that," I said. "That was my fiancé."

"Coras?" he asked.

I let out a laugh. "No, I'm not engaged to Coras but ..." I patted my thighs impatiently. "Can we get back rolling? I'm ready to lay another song."

"Okay. But I'd love to get you and Coras on a song together."

"Great. We can email him the track."

"Or he can come to New York and lay a song with you in the booth here in person. And then you guys can come down to the club and do a live show." His eyes lit up expectantly. "Can you make that happen? I'd be honored."

I wasn't sure if Coras would come, but I really wanted to see him. Lately, I'd been needing somebody to talk to concerning music and my self-doubt about creating good songs. Coras knew me best in that department. We had talked and left each other inboxes since I left home, but there was nothing like sitting across from him as he took my hands in his and made me believe I had the best voice in the world, past and present.

"I'll leave him a message after we finish recording," I said to DJ East, so as not to get his hopes up.

... Or my own.

Kirbie Amor > Coras Bane: Hey, homie. How would you like to come to New York and step in the booth with me? :) I met a DJ here named DJ East who's a fan of yours and wants us to do a track together and perform at his club. If you can't fly out here, I understand. I'll still email you the track so you can get on it. Get at me, boy.

CHAPTER 8

Coras Bane
outskirts of St. Joe, Missouri

Me and Ashleigh were on a road trip back from St. Joe, Missouri, which was only an hour away from Kansas City and might not technically have been considered a road trip but it sure felt like it. I was ready to climb in bed and go to sleep.

"Are you about to pass out on me?" Ashleigh asked from her spot behind the wheel. She had her seatbelt on, I didn't. "Did you get too high? Coras, wake up."

"I'm awake."

"I wanna celebrate when we get back home."

"What's to celebrate?"

"Are you kidding me? We got our biggest take-home pay yet!"

She was right. I had just performed at Missouri Western State University in front of over three thousand students and walked away with seventy-five hundred dollars. A quarter of it came from merchandise—I sold out of cotton tees with my name printed on it, which Ashleigh had convinced me to do. It was a good night, definitely.

But it was also a rare night, and I knew that the checks wouldn't always be this good. Before, I always had dope money to fall back on, a never-ending stream of street income that kept me afloat. But now I was at odds with my plug Milo Chavis, and therefore forced to depend on Ashleigh and rap money.

And both were fluctuating.

I was tempted to inbox Monifa and lay the dick on her in order to get back in good with Milo ... but I knew Gee would be beyond pissed. He took a bullet from one of Milo's goons and nearly lost his life.

That episode was still fresh on my mind. I had been banned from the Sprint Center and subsequently blackballed from other venues in Kansas City, which was why I had to travel out to St. Joe for work. In a way it was a good thing. It was a stimulus to seek gigs out of town again, which Ashleigh was doing a good job of booking.

Since Kirbie went to New York, Ashleigh had really been gung-ho.

With the passenger seat reclined, I put my forearm over my eyes to invite sleep. But then my cell phone made a beeping noise that indicated I had a Site notification.

I sat up slowly, using the Volvo's power seat controls.

"Look who's waking up to check The Site," Ashleigh said sarcastically when she saw me pull out my phone. "I thought you were tired."

I was still groggy as I thumbed my phone to open up the app. But when I saw I had a message from Kirbie I felt like I had been injected with a needle of hubba rock straight to the veins.

Kirbie I fucking miss you and I don't even miss people, I thought with a deep desire to be near her again, or at least in range of her scent.

I clicked on her message and began reading. It was a message inviting me to New York! I immediately started typing a reply and was surprised by how quickly she responded. I was happy and smiling like she was here in the car riding with us.

Coras Bane: I'm there! When can I come???

Kirbie Amor: As soon as you can get here

Coras Bane: I'll book a flight tonight

Kirbie Amor: Seriously?

Coras Bane: Damn right. I need to get out of KC anyway.

Kirbie Amor: Ashleigh won't let you LOL. She got you on a short leash

Coras Bane: I know how to wiggle out of it though

Kirbie Amor: LMAO!

Coras Bane: I'll see you soon then

Kirbie Amor: Okay. Call me when you have an idea when you'll land

Ashleigh must have leaned over and seen a part of what I was texting because she said, "Land where? What is that bitch talking about?"

I stuffed my phone in my pocket. "I need you to turn around."

"For what?"

"Airport. We're going to New York."

She flipped. "No you are not! We're going home."

"Kirbie just invited me out to New York. She said she got a show set up for me."

"Since when did she become your manager?"

"She's out there making moves and she wants me to be a part of it. This could be a big opportunity for me. La'Renz Taylor might see me perform and wanna sign me too."

"No, if he was gonna sign you he would've did it already. He heard your mixtape. That's how he found Kirbie. I think Kirbie wants you to come out there just to shove it in your face that she's doing better than you. She's not doing shit special, but she thinks she is."

"Kirbie doesn't get down like that. She's tryna get me some exposure."

"You're blinded, Coras. She's not to be trusted. Forget about her. She walked out on us, remember? If she makes it, she's not gonna bring you on with her."

"Ashleigh, take me to the airport."

"No." She had both hands on the wheel, focused on the road. "Who the fuck is she? You're not just dropping what you're doing and running to her whenever she calls. That's insane. She's not your woman. Only I have that privilege. You don't even have any clothes or luggage, a flight schedule ..."

"We can figure that out when we get to KCI. We're closer to the airport than your house. It'll take forever going out to Olathe then back out this way. Fuck clothes; I can go shopping in New York."

She shot me a look. "With Kirbie? Nigga please. If you go to New York I'm coming with you."

"I don't need you holding my fucking hand."

"If I can't go, then you're not going. And if you still try to go without me, then you better look for another place to stay when you get back. Because you won't be living with me. And how are you gonna go anyway with no money? The university deposited that check into my account, remember?"

I couldn't believe that just came out of her mouth. She had just threatened me. If it wasn't for the college's stipulation of direct deposit to performers, I would've had that seventy-five-hundred dollar payment in cash and wouldn't have needed Ashleigh to put it in her account. Now she was hanging that over my head, as well as threatening to kick me out. It reminded me of the shit that Monifa used to pull. Monifa threw it in my face all the time that she could make Milo stop supplying me and thus cut off my means of survival.

All these bitches are the same. They get leverage, then they get difficult.

"We're going to Olathe and we're gonna pack our things," Ashleigh stated. "Then we're gonna

find a flight. If all the flights going to New York are red-eyes, then we're waiting until the morning. No sense in pulling an all-nighter on a plane and limiting brain activity through sleep-deprivation just because Kirbie thinks it's important that you come now. She can wait, right?"

I bit my tongue.

CHAPTER 9

Kirbie Amor
Hunts Point, Bronx

"Why did you bring her?" I asked Coras, my hand a tight umbrella over the microphone. We were closed off in the booth together, surrounded by gray sound-absorbing foam panels, and I didn't want DJ East or Ashleigh—actually just Ashleigh—to hear what I was saying.

Coras whispered, "You didn't say she couldn't come."

"Really? That's your excuse? You brought her out to New York because I didn't say she couldn't come? You thought I'd want her to?"

"Kirbie, the girl is my manager."

This was a cop-out. I knew it was, because I knew Coras. He was afraid to admit that he didn't have a choice if Ashleigh came or not. She probably forced him to bring her somehow.

I turned and looked out the glass partition and saw Ashleigh staring at me with her arms crossed. Her eyes were digging into me with a jealous ferocity, and it was obvious that she felt entitled to hear our conversation. I knew it didn't help either that me and Coras were standing practically shoulder to shoulder, with my small shoulders inches shorter than his of course. I forgot how much I loved being close to him.

I kept the mic covered and smiled into Coras's ear from my tippy toes. "She's watching us."

"I know."

"I'm pissing her off right now by talking to you this close. I'm having fun doing it too." I mumbled incoherent gibberish in his ear and he chuckled. I laughed too. "I bet she thinks we're talking about something sexual."

I cut my eyes and saw Ashleigh shift her weight to the other foot, closing her crossed arms tighter. She was fuming.

Coras said, "Why pretend?" as his hand found my backside and squeezed hard, triggering an unexpected tightness in my pussy that gave my whole body a seismic jolt. It took everything in me not to cry out.

Only Coras's touch could cause this internal reaction from an ass grab.

"What kind of panties you got on?" he probed. "Any at all? I can't feel a panty line."

The height of the booth window and the wall it was framed in sat high, so neither Ashleigh nor DJ East could see what was going on in here below our waists.

So Coras's hand roamed over my plump derriere without consequence. "If we gon' make her mad, I wanna get something out of the deal."

"Okay, stop," I said, even though I didn't want him to. "You're taking it too far."

"Am I? Nah, *this* is too far," he said as his hand found a way inside the back of my jeans.

"Are you really doing this right now? *Quit it, Coras.*"

"Almost ... there."

I gasped—away from the microphone luckily.

He had wiggled his fingers between the split of my butt cheeks, where he met up with my womanly flower petals and began finger-feeling the silky wet texture. My pussy must have remembered him from the last time he invaded me, because it voluntarily opened up for him like an old friend reunited—*Come*

on in, my pussy seemed to say through its natural softening of its muscles.

It felt like a river poured out of me. I never would have thought that my first orgasm by Andre "Coras Bane" McDougald would have taken place while Ashleigh was watching. It felt amazing.

And then Archie popped in my mind. *Kirbie, you're engaged to me! I thought you was loyal!* And my subconscious reply was, *I thought so too.* But right now loyalty was only occupying a small part of my brain, while all that Coras stood for—mind, body, and his beautiful soul—became a monsoon, violently washing away every rational thought I ever had.

"Okay, guys. Sorry about the wait," came DJ East's voice through the intercom. "Every now and then I lose where I've saved and stored tracks. But I'm ready for you now. The next instrumental will be playing in three ... two ... one."

A second later it started streaming through our headphones, melodic and classical with soft kick drums intertwined. From the erotic fingering taking place inside my denim it sounded like victory music.

But then suddenly Coras's hand was gone like a thief in the night.

Recess was over.

Together, we churned out two great songs—one slow and ballad-y, the other upbeat and saturated with obnoxious bass that I was sure would be a hit in the night clubs. We were going for a third song, something tailored to perseverance in the street life that would resound with everyday folks from other walks of life, but we were cut off when La'Renz Taylor walked in the studio in a new three-piece suit.

His fine gentleman attire was in sharp contrast to the nasty mug on his face. He looked upset with me. Through the glass window, he jabbed two fingers at me and Coras and waved us both out of the booth.

"What's going on in here?" La'Renz questioned us when we were all standing near each other.

I frowned, trying to understand the problem. "We're busy making hits," I stated.

"See, that's the problem," La'Renz said combatively. "The only person that's supposed to be making hits in here is you, Kirbie."

"But this is a rapper I've been knowing for a long time," I explained. "He flew in to record a few songs with me. His name is Coras Bane. Coras, this is La'Renz Taylor."

Coras extended his hand. "Nice to meet you, Mr. Taylor."

La'Renz hesitated, as if he didn't want shake his hand. But he did.

Then Ashleigh butted in and introduced herself. "Ashleigh Hedgman. I'm Coras's manager."

La'Renz shook her hand as well, then said loudly, "I need everybody to step out of the studio for a minute so I can talk to Kirbie in private. Can I get you guys to do that for me, please?"

"You want me to leave too?" asked DJ East. He placed his hands on the arms of his swivel producer chair, unsure whether he should get up or not. "I don't have a problem with it. I'll step out too."

"If you would," La'Renz said.

My heart started beating faster. *What is going on here?*

When everyone was out of the room but me and La'Renz, he cocked his head to the side, assessing me. "Are you the boss?"

"No, I'm not," I said.

"Who's the boss?"

"You are. Why are you talking to me like this?"

"Because you don't invite people to the studio on *my time*."

"I'll pay for the time then."

He rubbed his forehead with his palm in frustration, bunching the skin up just below his perfect hairline. He grunted like he was having trouble getting through to me. "I don't wanna see anybody in the studio but you and the engineer. Unless I authorize it. Got it?"

"Why?"

"Because this is my mixtape you're putting out and I'm not letting just *anybody* feature on it."

"Coras isn't *anybody*. He's a well-known underground rapper. Google him."

"Key word: *underground*. Only famous rappers are going on this mixtape. It's your debut and I'm not going to let you fuck it up. We don't put our buddies and our friends on projects of this magnitude. This mixtape is a big fucking deal, and you need to realize that. I'm gambling my career on this project. This can make or break me, and it can make or break you too. I don't know how it's done in the Midwest, but here in New York we don't play favorites. We play smart."

"I'm offended by that."

"Well get used to it. Because it's an offensive industry."

CHAPTER 10

Kirbie Amor
Manhattan, New York

Back at the hotel in Manhattan, I found myself smoothing the wrinkles out of my fullsize bed in endless, tedious sweeps of my hand. Housekeeping had done a good job making it up, but I was just occupying time until La'Renz finished his talk. He was at the window with his back to me, on his cell phone with Sundi Ashworth.

When he hung up though, he continued to stare out the window. He was silent, focused, unmoving. I knew he was looking out at the Mount Eliyah ENT building, lost in another one of his vengeful trances.

I sat down on the bed, pulled my phone out and scrolled through The Site, clicking on a viral video here and there with the sound muted, as I decided to give La'Renz more time to himself. But I looked up after ten minutes and he was still standing there.

I was at a breaking point. I had too much on my mind. "La'Renz, I need to talk to you," I announced, placing my phone facedown on the bed.

He didn't respond right away. And when he did, he still didn't give me the respect of turning around to face me. He kept staring out the window rudely. "About?" he asked.

"My mixtape."

"*My* mixtape?"

"*Our* mixtape. It's not solely yours or mines. It's a collaborative effort." I was irritated. "I'm sorry to say that it might not ever get finished."

He turned to me then. It took a threat to get his attention. "And why wouldn't it get finished?"

"Because I don't know if I want to continue working on this project."

"You're under contract."

"I understand that. And if my friend Coras Bane and his producer Gee Beats can't be on my mixtape, then I'd like to entertain the idea of buying my way out of the contract."

"Do you have any idea what that number would be? You can't afford to buy your way out."

"You don't know me very well then."

"I *do* know you very well," he stated, crossing the room and standing at the base of the bed I was

sitting on. "You're just like any other female ruled by her emotions. You'll let your love for a nobody-ass rapper ruin the biggest opportunity you'll ever get in your lifetime."

"If you knew me, you'd know I was a loyal person and I don't turn my back on my friends."

"Typical female, like I said. You're gonna let your voice go to waste."

"It'll never be wasted. I can take my talent elsewhere."

"Not if I don't let you out of your contract."

"Nobody has ever made me stay somewhere I don't wanna be. And you won't be the first, sir."

La'Renz cracked his knuckles. It seemed like this was his way of intimidating me. But what he didn't know was that I had been the only girl in a room full of killers before. La'Renz was but one. I wasn't scared, not even a little bit. Maybe his dead wife Jazzmine Short was afraid to speak her mind, but I wasn't. And if he tried to drag me out the window onto the balcony and attempt to throw me off, then unlike Jazzmine he was coming with me.

Plus, I still had the .22 Ruger he gave me in my purse, which was sitting on the dresser.

Unzipped.

One long lean and I'd have it in my grasp.

Try me, nigga, I said to La'Renz with my eyes.

"You see that building across the street?" he asked me, pointing at the window he'd just come from. "There lies the fucking devil that sent me to prison for seven years. All I'm trying to do here is put forth the best possible product for me to shove in that muthafucka's face. It's selfish of me, Kirbie, I know, but that works in your favor. You know without a hair of a doubt that I want this mixtape to be the best that it can be. I'm not denying your rapper friend a spot on this disc because I don't like him or I think he can't rap. It's not personal against him. It's just that I have decades of experience, insight, and analytical data about this music business that no one else has. I know how to put together a piece that millions of people will buy."

I said, "That's understandable. And I feel where you're coming from. But you have to hear me out too. Coras is an asset to the project. He has his own fan base."

"I've never heard of him until today, Kirbie."

"So what? You're old."

He winced. "But I know who the rising stars are."

"Obviously you don't."

I grabbed my phone and stood next to him so he could see my screen with me. I showed him Coras's social media pages and the number of followers he had. I fingered through a few of his videos so La'Renz could see the viewcount—over a hundred thousand people had clicked to see and hear Coras perform. My phone started to lag as I searched for more proof, and I felt that La'Renz was losing patience, but I ended up finding photos of Coras's latest performance in St. Joe, Missouri. The faces in the crowd were predominantly white.

"He hustles harder than any rapper I know," I confessed.

La'Renz crossed his arms, sighing. He finally relented. "I'll let him on one song."

"Two songs," I pushed. "One is already produced by DJ East and the other has to be produced by my friend Gee Beats."

"One song, Kirbie."

"Two songs." I wasn't budging.

To further sell myself, I tapped play on one of the videos. It showcased Coras without a shirt, muscles glistening in sweat, holding his microphone out to a crowd of hundreds that sang his lyrics word for word with cult-like accuracy.

I saw a hint of a smile appear on La'Renz's face.

"So can we get two songs?" I asked him again.

He sighed for a second time, his arms still crossed, then looked down at his Italian black crocodile loafers as he rocked back and forth on his heels, contemplating an answer.

After a moment, he looked back at the video of Coras streaming on my phone and said, "Text that link to me." Then he started to head out of the hotel room. "I'm going to get a beer."

I smiled.

I take that as a yes!

CHAPTER 11

Coras Bane
Manhattan, New York

With a web-based notebook resting on my lap and the internet synced to the hotel's Wi-Fi, I typed in the website address to the nightclub me and Kirbie were supposed to be performing at tonight.

Ashleigh, who was leaning on my shoulder as we lay in the bed together, sucked her teeth when the club's homepage appeared on the screen. "It's not even a two-tiered club," she said, finding any fault she could. "What kind of shithole venue does Kirbie got us going to?"

I cut my eyes at her. "Why does it have to be two-tier?"

"The best clubs have multiple levels."

"But this is still a popular club. It says right here on their site that they have the number four biggest capacity in New York."

"Number four isn't number one."

I smacked my lips. "Why are you hating?"

"I'm not. I'm trying to figure out how Kirbie can get an interview on Revolt, which is reserved for celebrities only, but when it comes time to book a show for us she picks the number four club. Bitch, can we at least get number two? I know what she's doing. She's giving us the scraps. She doesn't want you performing at the bigger clubs because she doesn't want you outshining her."

"If she didn't want me outshining her, she wouldn't have invited me."

"She only invited you because she knew you'd bring me. She wants me to see how good she's doing but she ain't doing shit. I got a house out in Olathe, my own car, my own business and a fully-funded individual retirement account. She got a lot of catching up to do."

"Why are you competing with her?"

"I'm not. She's competing with me. She wants my life and she wants my man. She only wants you because you're with me. And that's fact, because she doesn't care about your rap career. She proved that today by booting you off the mixtape and kicking us out of the studio."

"That wasn't her doing. That was La'Renz's call."

"That's what she wants us to think. But she's just getting you back from the time you kicked her out of the studio. Remember?"

I would never forget the day Monifa stormed down into Gee's studio with a pistol in her purse, trying to shoot Kirbie with it after she caught us kissing. In the chaos, I made Kirbie leave instead of Monifa. It was a stupid choice.

But I still knew that incident had nothing to do with what happened at DJ East's studio today.

"Ashleigh, you got a fucked up way of thinking."

"No, my way of thinking is right on point. I have a way of seeing through people, seeing through the fake smiles and bullshit hospitality and discovering the master manipulator on the other side. Kirbie hates that I got that gift."

There was a knock on the door.

I gave Ashleigh my laptop and then I got up to answer it. When I turned the knob and opened it up, I was looking at a smiling Kirbie Amor.

"Hi, Coras," she said.

"Hey, wussup?"

"I got some good news." Her smile widened, and the first thing that popped in my mind was, *What, you left Archie and now you're here to give yourself to me?*

I said, "I love good news."

"Well ..." She paused for effect, trapping the tip of her tongue between her teeth. It was one of the sexiest gestures I'd ever seen her make. "I talked La'Renz into letting you back on the mixtape!"

My eyes got wide and I beamed a huge smile, giving her a little hug. I couldn't wait to show Ashleigh how wrong she was about Kirbie, so I invited her into our room.

"She got me back on the mixtape," I said to Ashleigh, who was still on the laptop checking out the night club.

She set the computer aside. "Why did she have to come in here for you to tell me that? I'm not even dressed."

Ashleigh had on a white hotel robe and red house shoes. She was technically dressed but she was presentable.

Kirbie said, "You're his manager so I wanted to make sure it was okay if Coras was featured on two songs."

"Two?" I said, impressed.

"Yep. Deuce."

Ashleigh said, "Can we get that in writing?"

"It's a mixtape," I said.

"And?" Ashleigh sat up some. "The music business is still a business. And I like to do business right."

"I don't have anything for you to sign," Kirbie said, still in good spirits. She wasn't letting Ashleigh get to her. "I can ask La'Renz if you want me to."

"Do that," said Ashleigh. "Don't come back making promises until you do."

Kirbie's politeness started to slip. I could see it in her eyes, in the way her back straightened.

Damn.

"Are you kicking me out of a hotel I paid for?" Kirbie said.

Ashleigh shot to her feet. "Honey, I can afford my own. If I would've paid for a room in this hotel, we'd be in a suite. Because I cash *checks*; I don't rely on drug money. So don't act like you're doing us a favor. Coras, get her."

"Ashleigh, chill out," I said.

"That's her smart ass, talking about this hotel like it's a five star. We should kick her ass out, just like they did us at that dingy ass studio. I've never had to cross train tracks to go to a studio. Have you, Coras? We need to be talking to La'Renz directly anyway. She's just a messenger."

I knew where this was going. So I told Ashleigh that me and Kirbie would talk about the details of the mixtape between ourselves, alone, and I'd let her know the plan later. She made a fuss about it, mainly because she didn't want me and Kirbie leaving the hotel room alone, so I told her we were just stepping outside onto the balcony.

As soon as we got out there, I felt an icy chill in the wind and saw Kirbie rubbing her arms to keep warm. I wanted to put my arms around her but ...

"I just wanna fight Ashleigh one good time," Kirbie said. "I don't wanna kill her, just fuck her up real good." She rested her elbows on the railing, looking up at the night sky. Very little stars out tonight, just a cold breeze. She rubbed her arms again, so I leaned on the railing next to her to block some of the wind. "Now Monifa on the other hand ... what her brother did to Gee ... I know I'ma end up killing her one day."

"No you ain't," I said.

"Why ain't I?"

"Because I won't let you."

"Why are you still protecting Monifa?"

"I'm not. I'm protecting you and yo career. Stop thinking like a gangster. Start thinking like a superstar."

"Okay, I'ma hire somebody to do it."

I laughed.

Then the sliding glass door came open behind us, and both me and Kirbie turned to look. Ashleigh was standing in the doorway.

"I'm about to get in the shower," she said to me.

"Okay," I replied flatly.

"Are yall gon' be out here long?"

"Probably."

She gave me a look, as if she wanted to say something about how buddy-buddy close I had leaned toward Kirbie. But for some reason she didn't. Then she slid the glass door closed again. But when me and Kirbie turned back toward the sky, I was almost certain I heard the door *click*.

Kirbie heard it too. "Did that bitch just lock us out here?"

"I think so."

"Does she really think we would try to sneak out of the hotel room while she's in the shower?"

"She's been acting out of character lately."

"Leave her," Kirbie said, as if it was that simple.

"Leave her for who?" I said back.

Kirbie didn't reply, because she knew I was flirting.

I changed the subject. "How'd you convince La'Renz to let me back on the mixtape?"

"I told him I quit if you can't be on there."

"You didn't."

"I did. I'm not turning my back on you and Gee."

"Kirbie, you can't do that shit here. La'Renz will really let you go. Don't blow it. You might not get another chance."

"I'm not gonna let him walk all over me. My name is gonna be on this mixtape. I deserve some say-so."

I nodded, smiling inside, then said, "Thank you for standing up for yourself and putting me on there."

"You're welcome. I know you'd do the same for me."

She looked across the street at the Mount Elijah ENT building and I stared with her, in silence, loving this time out of town with the woman I loved. Then for no reason at all she leaned over the railing dangerously, the top bar pushing into her stomach now, and I tensed up, knowing she was safe but ready to grab her if the metal gave out.

"How far down do you think this is?" she asked me.

"This railing wasn't built to be leaned on, Kirbie. Cut it out."

"How far?"

"This is the eighth floor. Eight stories."

"How many feet is in a story?"

"I don't know. Ten, fifteen."

She planted her feet and leaned back up. *Thank God.* Staring across the street again, she said, "The news people said Jazzmine Short fell from a height about ten times as high as this. That's a fucked up way to go."

"Not necessarily. I'm sure she died on impact, pain-free."

"But look how long it took for her to hit the ground. What was going through her head as she was falling? That had to be horrible."

I shrugged one shoulder, uninterested. I didn't care about Jazzmine Short. I cared about Kirbie Amor. I still had her scent on my fingertips. Like an addict, I kept rubbing my nose to get a whiff (however faint), torturing myself. To make matters worse, I imagined her bent over the railing again, me slowly easing in behind her. A shudder went through me just thinking about it.

"Cold?" Kirbie asked me.

"Nah ... uh, yeah, a little bit. You?"

"It doesn't even matter. We can't get in until yo girlfriend open the door."

I looked back. I could see the bathroom door was still closed, steam vapors pumping through the cracks, and I figured that Ashleigh was still bathing in another one of her long showers. As I turned back toward the street below, I stole a peek at Kirbie's irresistible booty filling out her stretch denim. It was unreal how defined she was.

Damn Kirbie why do you have to be so fucking flawless, so sexy without trying?

My dick was pulsing painfully.

"Do you think he did it?" Kirbie asked me.

"Who did what?"

"La'Renz. Do you think he killed Jazzmine Short? Or do you think Eliyah did it and set La'Renz up?"

"If La'Renz did kill her, I think it was an accident. Maybe they were arguing and they got into a little shoving match and she went up and over."

"An accident? I don't think so."

"Did you ask La'Renz if he killed her?"

Her mouth hung open, as if my question was completely ridiculous. I could see all the way down her throat now, the wet moisture in and around her

tongue glistening. Primal, erotic thoughts of fellatio took control of my mind.

As if my dick wasn't already hard enough ...

"I'd never ask him that," she said.

"Do *you* think he did it?"

She got quiet, then said, "I think he could have done it. Since I've been around him, I've seen what kind of temper he can have. I've seen exactly why they call him Buddy Rough. One minute I feel like he's like a brother I never had, the next minute I don't trust him."

"Do you trust *me?*" I asked.

She stared in my unblinking eyes quizzically, unsure of what I was getting at. But when I glanced in the room—two quick glances to prompt her to look with me—she followed my eyes and saw that I was telling her that Ashleigh was still showering, that we shouldn't let this moment go to waste.

She took a step back, away from me. "No, Coras. Not here. She can come out any min—"

I gathered her in my arms and pulled her to the only side of the balcony that was concealed by the sliding door's thermal black curtains. I could hear in her breathing that she wanted me, but her body was pulling away.

"Coras, I can't," she said. "I have a fiancé."

"We don't have time for excuses," I said in frustration, as I held her snug to my chest. It was criminal of me to be holding her this tight, against her will, but I didn't give a fuck. "You already let me play wit' that pussy and leaked on my fingers. It's too late. You already signed up for this."

I lowered my mouth to hers and kissed her. She let out a submissive breath of air and let me suck her wet tongue. The blood in my heart was pounding; hers too, I could feel it. She groaned softly in my mouth, then suddenly her hand was cupping my testicles, groping the length of me, which was full and primed.

She's sex-starved, I realized.

And I knew here and now that she and Archie would never share a passion as strong as ours. I knew before, but now it was written.

I took her lips more aggressively, knowing we didn't have much more time. My mating instincts ached badly. Unsafely. If Ashleigh hadn't been nearby, if I didn't need that bitch financially or legally, I would have long-dicked Kirbie until every deep place in her body came completely undone.

I heard a tiny cry escape her lips when I pulled away. And I couldn't pull away very far because she had my shirt wrapped in her fist.

"That's all I wanted," I said to her. "We'll continue this another time, okay? Let my shirt go, fam."

CHAPTER 12

Sammy "The Hitman" Russtrip
Manhattan, New York

I had been gazing across the street at an aged man playing a soft tune on his acoustic guitar outside a storefront, his brown felt hat laying beside him upturned. You could see the tail of a lonely dollar bill or two flapping inside.

There were a few telltale signs that told me this man wasn't an ordinary sidewalk beggar, but rather a musician whose artistry hadn't been commercialized. One sign was the condition of his guitar—it was boldly new-looking with a shiny wood finish. Another sign was the way in which he strummed the strings; he was carefree and graceful in the downstroke of his thumb, producing a mellowing sound that had passersby smiling on.

"Oh, that's a fucking letdown if I ever saw one," said my son Jarvis, who was looking through the eyecups of my high-resolution binoculars.

"Fucking scaredy cats had time to make it happen. Dammit ... just when the stakeout was getting good ..."

I turned quick, snatching the binoculars from him. It wasn't often I got distracted away from a target, and it really had me angry. Discipline in this line of work was life or death.

It was my own fault. *Tighten up, Sammy,* I told myself.

Through the binocular lenses I saw Kirbie Amor standing a foot or two away from a male I didn't recognize. I adjusted the binocular's center focus wheel, enhancing the clarity, and witnessed a knot of anguish appear on Kirbie's face.

"What did I miss?" I asked, as I observed every action the two were making on the balcony.

"Kirbie was about to get fucked on the eighth floor," Jarvis said.

"We need to find out who that black male is and document it."

"I already know who that is. It's Coras Bane."

I lowered the binoculars and frowned at my son. "How do you know?"

"The Site." He wiggled his smartphone at me. "They're social media friends, but from what happened up there, we know they're more than that.

And it's so scandalous because Kirbie is engaged to a nigga named Archie Waters in Kansas City. But Coras is a Kansas City rapper who used to record with Kirbie. Coras is Kirbie's side nigga, apparently. I would've never guessed that Kirbie was a ho."

"You know all this through The Site?"

"Yes, *Sammy!*"

He said my name with sarcasm, because he'd rather be calling me "daddy." But I loathed the word *daddy*, especially while out in the field. "Father" was less bitchy, but it was still inappropriate.

"That's why I'm always on my phone. I'm putting pieces together," he said. "I can find out more in thirty seconds than you can in thirty days. There's another girl in the hotel room, her name is Ashleigh Hedgman. She's Coras's manager and also his girlfriend. That's why Coras and Kirbie hurried up and stopped kissing. They didn't want to get caught. There's a big triangle—or rectangle—of sexual deceit going on."

"Don't get thrown off track. The main target is La'Renz."

"I know. But look how much I found out. That's why you shouldn't be so against the internet. Now is it okay if I look at my phone from time to time?"

"No."

I lifted the binoculars and found Kirbie again. It startled me—because she was looking directly at me, or my car. It was dumb of me though to have even been jumpy; Kirbie couldn't make me out from this far away, and it was impossible for her to see through the tints.

I continued to spy, until the balcony's sliding door opened up and a light-complexioned woman appeared in a bath robe, her hair long and water-wet. I assumed this was the Ashleigh Hedgman female that my son just spoke of. I handed him the binoculars to confirm, and he did, then handed them back. Ashleigh was a beautiful woman too. Her eyes were narrow and fierce, and her demeanor seemed to command respect. She was the type of woman I had always favored, back when I used to let the evils of love rule my life.

When Ashleigh, Coras, and Kirbie disappeared inside, I scanned the facade of the hotel until I got to La'Renz's balcony. His curtains were closed, lights off. Normally at this time he would be staring across the street at the Mount Eliyah headquarters.

"Did you see La'Renz turn in?" I asked.

"Yeah, he went to sleep."

"You sure?"

"Positive."

My phone rang. I handed the binoculars back to my son and fished my cell out of my pocket.

"This is Sammy," I answered.

"I need you to pull out of there and head to Sundi's house," said Rose, who was an old Spanish woman that worked more in Eliyah's mansion than in the field.

"I'm at the hotel watching La'Renz," I told her. "He's first priority."

"Well I'm telling you to go watch Sundi. We need to see every action she takes while she's still under the impression that she's getting her job back."

"Did Eliyah authorize this?"

"Yes! I wouldn't be telling you to do it if he didn't!"

I steeled myself against calling Rose out of her name. She assumed because she was pushing sixty and was one of the first female Hispanic military pilots in the Air Force, she had the right to talk to a third generation investigator any kind of way. But how much experience did she have in murder and not just flying planes? Her daily activity consisted of strutting around Eliyah's Brooklyn mansion in tasteless track suits barking orders at me. Seven

years ago when I worked for La'Renz, I dealt with La'Renz directly. There was no senior citizen as the middleman.

Yesterday is gone. Tomorrow has not yet come. We have only today. Let us begin, I mused, reciting Mother Teresa silently.

Then I hung up on Rose without the courtesy of a goodbye.

CHAPTER 13

Milo Chavis
Los Angeles, California

I was standing in an alley blindfolded. This was something I never thought I would've done voluntarily but ... here I was, somewhere in Los Angeles, California, blind, nervous, and waiting for instructions. My righthand man Oyeah Mason was here with me—or so I thought. I hadn't heard him speak since Mark Beltrán, who was my *OG Tahoe* connection, picked us up from the airport and brought us here and tied a rag over our eyes for "security reasons."

This is bullshit, I thought.

"Oyeah, when's the last time you been blindfolded?" I asked just to make sure he was still here with me.

Oyeah chuckled. "Grade school. Field Day."

"*Sssh,*" said Mark, hushing us. "Here they come."

I heard a screen door open and a man's voice, in Spanish, ask some kind of question to Mark, who answered back in the same dialect. Then, in English, Mark told us that he'd be waiting outside for us after our meeting was over.

This is bullshit.

I felt hands grab onto me and usher me inside a building that was unmistakably in the business of serving food. I could smell seasoning in the air, hear a gas burner igniting (we were in a kitchen), before I was eventually brought to a room where I was seated at a table and left there.

I was startled when I felt a hand touch my thigh under the table. I swatted it away immediately.

"Just making sure you're still there," Oyeah said. "Making sure they didn't separate us."

"Keep your fucking hands away from me, nigga," I said with humor in my voice, but overwhelmingly relieved that he was still near.

This meeting wasn't necessarily by choice. For the most part I was forced to come to California. Since Coras stopped buying *OG Tahoe* from me, things had went bad. Coras had been my biggest serve, roughly 75 percent of my gross profit, and when he refused to cop from me after the shooting incident at the Sprint Center, I could no longer afford to purchase my normal bundle. And there was no "buy less product" option, Mark informed me. It was either I afford the normal amount, or I got nothing at all. It wasn't Mark's rules. It was the *familia's*. And in order for me to be an exception to the rule, I had to meet with the head of the family in person and explain my situation. In simple terms, I needed time to build up my clientele to replace what I lost in Coras.

I was in the hot seat right now. And this was a foreign thing to me, because I was usually the one putting niggas in the hot seat for fucking up my money.

Then my phone vibrated in my pocket and startled me.

Mark had told me and Oyeah to turn our phones completely off before we came inside but I opted for mute mode. I knew it was my sister Monifa calling again with the same questions—*Are you okay? Have you made up with Coras yet? Have you talked to him? Can you tell Coras I'm sorry when you hear from him?* I blamed Monifa for me even being here, that bitch. The actual person who shot Coras's partner, a guy that worked for me named Mario Powell, was just supposed to film a routine beat down, not

attempt to kill. Last I heard he was hiding out, from Coras and me.

My phone kept buzzing. And I figured I had a minute or two before the meeting started so I eased it out of my pocket, resting it on my lap clandestinely. I wanted to text Monifa and let her know what city I was in just in case something went wrong, but when I used my finger to lift the blindfold a smidge, I got the shock of my life.

There were already several mean-looking Mexicans sitting at the table with us!

I thought I could put the blindfold back down and everything would be alright but before I could fully cover my eyes I saw two or three of the bigger Mexicans get excited, in a bad way. Loud Spanish was thrown around, I heard someone's chair screech back, and then I felt Oyeah's hand on my thigh again, a gesture that said, *What's going on?* I put my hand on top of his in reply. *Whatever happens let's stick together.*

Then a punch came from left field.

Bam!

It rocked me so hard the two left legs of my chair came off the ground and I smacked the floor sideways. I heard Oyeah cursing, and then his voice was muffled after someone put something over his mouth. A chaotic argument ensued amongst the Mexicans in Spanish, everyone trying to out-talk each other, and for a split second I thought I might've been able to escape. But I didn't even have a chance to get up, as someone dragged me across the floor and slung me against a wall. Hard. The back of my head had to be bleeding, I wasn't sure. My blindfold was still intact, and I was too scared to remove it. And then a sack swooped down over my head, darkening my world from a permeable black to an abysmal black robbed of all hope. The sack's drawstring yanked tight and threatened to suffocate me. But there was a mouth hole. I could breathe.

Barely.

Then came the *click-clack* of a handgun, one of the worst sounds you could hear with no eyesight.

A new commanding voice entered the room, speaking in English: "Why are my guests on the floor?"

Everyone seemed to be speaking at once. My heart was racing. Then I got a sudden start when the new man's voice spoke to me from right in front of my face.

"Milo, correct?"

He had to be squatting in front of me. "Yes, I'm Milo," I answered.

"Why did you remove your blindfold?"

"My phone, I was—a call came through—"

"Why was your phone even on?"

I didn't have an answer.

"Let me tell you something, *el amigo*," he said to me in a condescending tone. "My name is Julian Beltrán. I am your god, therefore you do not break my rules, and if you do—which you have done—then you lose heaven. You've just lost heaven, *vato*. I was going to consider providing you with kilos of *mota* on consignment. That deal is now off the table."

I couldn't get my words out fast enough. "Wait, Mr. Beltrán, I've been dealing with Mark for years—"

"Shut the fuck up!" he barked so loud it made me flinch. "You broke the rules. Not me, *you!* So what you need to do is get the fuck out of my restaurant, go back to the fucking ghetto you came from and scrounge up the money to pay for the *mota* in full. That's what you do, okay?"

I nodded. "Yes, sir."

There was no sense in arguing. If Julian Beltrán was anything like I'd heard—callous, money-driven, a dominator in Hollywood's drug scene—then I'd take it as a blessing that he was still willing to work with little ol' me. I'd come up with a way to get every penny Julian required, with or without Coras.

But preferably with.

Suddenly, I felt two men on either side of me lifting me by my armpits. As I was being carried out still blindfolded, I was thinking about how I could get Coras back on my team ...

CHAPTER 14

Coras Bane
outskirts of St. Louis, Missouri

Me and Ashleigh were leaving St. Louis, Missouri. We were thirty miles into a hundred-twenty-mile drive west to Columbia, Missouri, where I had another show to do tonight. It had been months since the shooting at the Sprint Center but I *still* couldn't book a gig in Kansas City. Promoters still had me labeled high-risk, because word around town was that me and Milo had yet to settle our differences, that we were from two different 'hoods trying to kill each other. But I wasn't looking for him. And he wasn't looking for me … to my knowledge. He had my number, I had his.

But since the streets thought we were at odds, traveling to fans in surrounding cities to get paid was the norm now.

I thought about going further out—like Texas, Ohio, North Carolina, Colorado, a few locales where my fanbase was strong—but I just couldn't handle more than two or three hours in the same car as Ashleigh. Ever since I made her my girl officially, all she did was bitch about Kirbie. Kirbie ain't this, Kirbie thinks she's that. Ashleigh didn't complain this much as a side chick when I was with Monifa.

Even now, as we sailed along a two-lane highway in this new Porsche Cayenne (a mid-size luxury crossover SUV that Ashleigh would never admit she bought impulsively from her insecurity about Kirbie), she was talking *at* me in frustration over me still being friends with Kirbie.

I didn't want to hear it. I was letting it go in one ear and out the other, as I sat with an elbow out the window looking at my phone, enjoying a texting conversation with Gee Beats.

> **Gee Beats:** Where R U now?
>
> **Coras Bane:** Still a few miles out from Columbia.
>
> **Gee Beats:** Is Ashleigh getting on your nerves yet? Lol
>
> **Coras Bane:** I wish you and Kirbie was on the road with me. I could tolerate her then. When can you start traveling again?

Gee Beats: All my physical therapy will be done next week. Doctor said I'll be good to go.

Coras Bane: I'm not gonna let you drink on the road this time. I'm serious, bro.

Gee Beats: Yes you will. Because pretty soon Ashleigh is gonna make you an alcoholic too.

Coras Bane: LMAO!

Gee Beats: Bottoms up

Coras Bane: LMMAO!

"Why are you smiling?" Ashleigh asked me. "Are you texting Kirbie?"
"No, I'm not."
"You are too. Let me see your phone."
I frowned and stopped paying her any attention, as I typed in another comment to Gee.

Coras Bane: Fuck it drinks on me when I get back to KC

Gee Beats: Lol #mynigga #denzelvoice And next time you talk to Kirbie let her know I put together a dope instrumental for you and her to lace.

Coras Beats: Okay. Last time I talked to her she said she could only get you one production credit on her mixtape. But she let La'Renz Taylor hear your sounds and he was so impressed that—

Ashleigh tried to snatch my phone in the middle of my text but my reflexes were too quick.

"What the fuck are you doing?!" I snapped.

"Show me who you're texting."

"No."

"If you don't show me your phone, we're not going to Columbia. I'll call the promoter and cancel."

Another threat. I felt ice running through my veins.

"This is yo car," I said. "Go wherever you wanna go. I'm just riding."

"So you're just gonna blow me off? I'm tired of you treating me like you treated Monifa."

"Well stop acting like her then."

This struck her hard. She froze, and I wasn't sure what was going through her head but I knew without a doubt that she was hurt—and she deserved to be hurt.

My elbow was still resting on the window, as I turned my head into the blustering wind of the highway. I loved feeling the wind on my face during long drives. But then I felt the glass of the window under my arm and I pulled my elbow inside. Ashleigh was rolling all the power windows up at once. Then she engaged the safety locks.

Petty ass bitch, I thought. *She's trying to force me to argue with her.*

"So were you and Kirbie texting about me?" she asked.

"I already told you I wasn't texting her."

"Let me see then."

I shook my head no. "You need to start trusting me more."

"You haven't earned my trust."

"Well why are you with me then?"

I was challenging her to leave me, which would make my life easier in some respects. But truth was I needed her. She was a damn good business woman and knew how to talk to people in that polished professional manner. The challenge was a bluff to get her to shut the fuck up.

It worked.

She turned the wheel into the next rest stop, got out and went into the women's restroom. I reached over and tapped a button on the arm of her door, releasing the locks on the windows and rolled mines down again. Then I sat with my back against the leather, thinking about how much money I would have in my pocket right now if I was still selling *OG Tahoe*. I wouldn't be so dependent on Ashleigh. I had been tolerating shit from her that I wouldn't have tolerated under normal circumstances.

Then my cellphone rang, and my first thought was that it was Ashleigh calling from the toilet. But it was Milo Chavis.

I answered it. "Yeah, wussup?"

"Hey, Coras, wussup."

"You tell me."

"Aw, nothing. Just got off the phone with my sister Monifa. All she ever does is ask for shit. One favor after another. I see why yall got into that altercation at the studio."

He said it like it wasn't a big deal anymore. *Why the sudden change?*

I said, "So wussup? Why are you calling me out the blue?"

"Well, I just came from out west, LA and shit. I'm in the town now with a surplus. I figured I'd forgive you for the little incident with my sister if you can overlook what happened to yo boy and we can focus on getting money again. And for the

record, the person who shot him ain't on my team no more. I'm looking for him just like you are."

"I'm not apologizing."

He got quiet. "Okay, well I'll apologize. I never intended for anybody to get seriously injured."

"You'll have to apologize to my nigga Gee, not me."

"Is he around?"

"Nah. But look ... I'm not in the area right now. I'm headed to Columbia. If you wanna talk about money we'll talk later."

"I won't be able to work with you on this package that just came in. But if you give me your money now, then I'll show you love on my next trip."

"We'll talk later," I said again.

After I hung up with Milo, I looked over and saw Ashleigh headed back to the car. She climbed back in, sliding on her seatbelt.

Then she looked at me with puffy red eyes. She had been crying. She said, "Show me your phone or we're going back to Kansas City right now and you're getting your shit out of my house and I'm never speaking to you again."

A tear dropped from her eye, which she quickly swiped away.

I sighed. With the potential of having Milo back as a supplier, I needed all the money I could get so I could cop as much weed as possible, guaranteeing I wouldn't need shit from Ashleigh ever again as long as I kept my financial rotation in order. The proceeds from this show in Columbia were more important than ever. I needed every penny.

And Ashleigh had the rock. For now.

I handed her my phone and she looked at my latest texts. I'm sure she wasn't pleased that me and Gee were teasing about her, but she didn't mention it as she scrolled through our exchange. She handed me my phone back, then started up the Porsche.

"That's all you had to do in the first place," she said. "Stop testing me, Coras."

***

I was sitting in the parking lot by myself, in the driver's seat of Ashleigh's Porsche. I took her car keys after she fell asleep, and now I was sitting here in the dark, under the moon, trying to get my thoughts together. I was questioning the direction of my life.

I thought my rap career would have taken off by now. Granted, I had a huge underground

following and a couple features on Kirbie's upcoming mainstream mixtape, but there was still no guarantee that I would get famous off of my musical talent. I didn't want to be one of those people who called themselves a rapper but wasn't able to fully capitalize on the business end.

And that was part of the reason I was here parked in front of Monifa's place.

I could get by just fine copping dope from Milo without getting involved with Monifa again, but I sort of missed that loud-mouthed chick. She always promoted and shared my music on her Site page, and in bed she didn't mind being un-ladylike. She loved fucking. Her only hang-up was shooting cum on her, whereas Ashleigh had a *list* of things she wouldn't do.

Mind made up, I took my keys—or Ashleigh's keys—out of the ignition. Monifa didn't know I was here. This was going to be a surprise.

I climbed out the Porsche, locked it with the keypad and crossed the parking lot. I had my hands in my pockets as I walked up her steps, feeling a little nervous as if this was a first date. *What if she has company?* I thought.

I knocked on her door anyway.

When it opened and she saw me for the first time in months—other than the Site pictures I uploaded, all of which she had affectionately Liked—her face lit up into an ever-widening smile.

Then she screamed like she hit the lottery.

Monifa Chavis: I knew he would come back to me! There's nothing like being in a relationship with the man you're meant to be with. I won't let him go this time. No way, no how.

CHAPTER 15

Kirbie Amor
Atlanta, Georgia

My very first day in Atlanta, Georgia, would never be forgotten. In the back of the limousine as me and La'Renz left the airport, he leaned forward from the opposite seat and handed me an envelope.

"Open it," he instructed, smiling as I looked it over front and back for a name. There was no label anywhere. "Just open it. It's yours. Would you rather I write your name on the front next time?"

I worked my fingernail underneath the seal, tearing it an inch at a time. *Rip, rip, rip.* I was nervous.

He said, "I told you signing with me would be the best decision you ever made."

Inside the envelope was a Taylor Music Group business check worth $25,000. Written on the memo line was *Performance Royalties* in La'Renz's handwriting. This was my biggest music check ever!

It didn't come close to the type of money I'd seen in the drug game, but it was a start.

Legal money, I thought to myself, genuinely pleased. I couldn't wait to tell Coras.

My excitement came through in my smile, and I was still looking at the lengthy spelling of the dollar amount when I told La'Renz thank you.

Then he took the check back, placed it back inside the jagged rips of the envelope and put it in the inside pocket of his suit jacket.

"I'll keep it safe for you until it's time to cash it," he said.

"When can I cash it?" I asked.

"After your obligations are met."

I-85 took us to our next destination, which was a Falcon's game where I was scheduled to sing the National Anthem—yes, me, the freaking *National Anthem* on live television. As La'Renz helped me out of the limo, photographers blinded us with camera flashes and a barrage of questions. I felt La'Renz's hand go around my waist as he pulled me close and we smiled and posed together.

As we turned to be led inside by security, a woman photographer's question stood out to me among the noise of the rest.

"Hey, La'Renz!" she yelled. "Jazzmine Short's first performance was at a Falcon's game. Are you trying to lead Kirbie in Jazzmine's footsteps?"

I looked back to see the woman's face but all I got was more bright lights that made me quickly turn away. But even when I was standing on the green turf of the fifty yard line holding the microphone and singing passionately in front of the nation, that question still lingered: *Are you trying to lead Kirbie in Jazzmine's footsteps?*

The applause for my performance was mesmerizing. I waved at everyone as I left the field, and as soon as I made it to the hallway where La'Renz was supposed to be waiting for me, I froze in shock when I saw who he was talking to.

My idol, Caylene Hope.

She had a Falcons jersey on, the strap of her tote bag slanting across the front of her, and my first fanatic thought was, *She carries her own bag?* There was only one photographer taking pictures of La'Renz and Caylene as they spoke amicably, probably a personal photographer hired by Caylene. Slowly, I approached them, and finally Caylene glanced my way and smiled.

"Hi, Kirbie," she beamed, and opened her arms for a hug. I was shaking when we embraced.

She was treating me like an old friend and I didn't know why. Then I remembered the friend request she sent me on The Site, which I had accepted. Did that mean we were real friends?

"Hi," I said back nervously.

"You rocked that anthem. Didn't she, La'Renz?"

"Best I ever seen," he replied like a proud father.

I thanked them both, then asked Caylene the first question that came to mind. "What are you doing here?"

She laughed, so did La'Renz and a few others standing nearby.

"I'm a Falcons fan," she said.

I felt like an idiot. That was basic information in her biography.

A man standing behind her whispered in her ear and she told me and La'Renz that she had to go to her seat while the route was still clear. I wanted to ask her so many more questions—*Are you mad at me for singing one of your songs on my first Revolt interview? Did you know that my dad is one of your biggest fans? Did you know* I'm *one of your biggest fans?*—but I opted to remain silent as she gave La'Renz a light goodbye hug and a quick pat on his back.

She turned to me. "You got a phone?"

I nodded eagerly. "Yes."

"Let's take a selfie together. You can upload it to The Site and tag me in it. Okay?"

I did just that, uploading the pic under the caption: *Me standing next to the best who ever did it.*

Just as I was about to say goodbye to her, she put her arm around my shoulder and pulled me close, whispering, "Be careful of the company you keep. Don't trust him. Don't end up like Jazzmine."

Then she was off, and I was stuck there for a moment watching Caylene and her entourage march away, trying to process what she just told me.

Back in the limo I was sitting in silence and so was La'Renz, but he was texting somebody and I was just staring at him purposefully, as the driver got us back on the road. I wanted to ask La'Renz the same question that the lady in the crowd of paparazzi had asked—*Are you trying to lead me in Jazzmine's footsteps?*—but La'Renz suddenly got a phone call that turned out to be an interview for me from an Atlanta radio personality. I was on speakerphone answering questions for an hour. And when the limo turned into the semi-circle of the main entrance of a high-end Atlanta hotel, I looked at La'Renz in confusion.

"We're staying in another hotel?" I asked.

"Yes," he said, fastening the two buttons on his suit jacket. Then he sat back against the seat and waited for the driver to open our door. "It's a five-star hotel, more prestigious than the one we had in Manhattan. You'll like this one better."

"I thought you bought a mansion down here."

"I did. But it's not ready for us yet. Renovations, you know?"

No, I didn't know.

Our room had two beds, same as in New York. But this one was bigger, the AC was cooler, and then there was the most important thing—there was no Mount Eliyah ENT across the street. La'Renz removed his shirt and headed for the shower, not offering to let me shower first.

I had a lot on my mind—and I was going to share it with him as soon as he was done.

In the meantime, I sat down on my bed and pulled out my phone, logging into The Site. I couldn't wait to read the comments from my selfie with Caylene Hope.

Makea WorkingWoman Price: You guys could pass for twins!

Shan Lovingmeandhim Joseph: Wonderful singing at the game, Kirbie! You're rendition of the National Anthem gave me goosebumps! #starinthemaking

ChiTown Millie Walker: Get away from her, Caylene! She's trying to steal your shine! #snakesinthegrass #kirbiedoesntcompare #rookieversusveteran

Usef FactsNotHate Booker: This looks like a before and after picture.

Mellie NoTurningBack Godder: Cute pic! If I didn't know any better, I'd say you two were sisters

ChromeGat OaklandStyle99: ^^Sisters? They're nowhere close in age. More like mother and daughter or auntie and niece.

Danny DoDirt: Who the fuck is Kirbie Amor? Caylene, why are you cosigning her?

One of the comments caught my attention. It was the mother and daughter comparison. It made me think about what my father said a little while ago during a horrible argument with Archie. My father blurted out that my mother was—not had been, but *was*—one of the most successful women in the music industry. Why did he say that? Was he talking about Caylene Hope? Could she really be my mother? Or was my father just lying to Archie to make himself feel better about running my real mother off?

The more I thought about Caylene Hope as my mom, the more the idea seemed totally ridiculous.

I pressed the app's back-arrow, which took me to my newsfeed. At the top was a popular post from someone I should have deleted a long time ago—Monifa Chavis. Her post read:

> **Monifa Chavis:** I knew he would come back to me! There's nothing like being in a relationship with the man you're meant to be with. I won't let him go this time. No way, no how.

It seemed as though Monifa had found her an old flame. I was glad for her. Now she could stay out of Coras's life and fuck up somebody else's. The status was sitting at 99 Likes. I clicked Like, giving her 100.

Good for you, Monifa. Now you can stay the hell away from Coras.

I started to call Coras, tease him a little bit, ask him if he was jealous that Monifa moved on from him so quick, but La'Renz walked out of the shower in the nude, drying his hair with a big white gold-embroidered bath towel. His penis dangled between his legs, and it was so gigantic all I could do was stare at it in shock. Its girth was unreal. Bigger than anything I'd ever seen in person.

"One of the best showers I had since I've been free," La'Renz said.

I couldn't stop staring.

Once, when I was watching a porno with Archie, there was an actor who was just as big, but Archie told me that it wasn't real; it was all camera tricks, angles, and lighting.

"You're up, Kirb," he said to me, as he bent at the knees to dry his balls.

Did he just call me *Kirb*? Did he really think we were at this point in our relationship, this comfortable with each other to hand out nicknames and expose body parts, especially in a business relationship?

He sat down on the bed, his back to me. Then he turned my way, laying a leg on the bed, and there it was again—his private length. "Don't turn the water all the way to the left. It gets scalding hot."

I grew up in the streets so my instincts were fine-tuned, at least I liked to think so. And right now my instincts were telling me that I was being toyed with. Maybe La'Renz thought I'd be so impressed with his size that I'd automatically jump on top of

him. Perhaps this was how he won Jazzmine over. I didn't know his motive, and I didn't care.

Don't trust him. Don't end up like Jazzmine. Caylene Hope's words were still fresh on my mind.

I grabbed my shampoo and soap and stalked toward the shower—without glancing his way. I locked the bathroom door before I undressed.

After I was done and all dried off, lotioned, and in my tee and mini sleep shorts, I unlocked the door and stepped out, prepared to have a long conversation with La'Renz about the direction of my career.

But he was laying underneath the covers, sound asleep.

CHAPTER 16

Kirbie Amor
Kansas City, Missouri

I was back in Kansas City, at KCI airport, waiting on the carousel to swing my Northface backpack around. All I had was that one bag. I had bought a lot of clothes since I started working with La'Renz, but he wouldn't let me wear the same thing twice, so everything I owned could fit inside the backpack. "Everyday has to be something new," he had said to me. "Wear it and throw it away. Only ordinary people repeat outfits. Ordinary is career suicide."

Truth was, I rarely ever wore the same thing twice anyway.

I was home as a "vacay." La'Renz told me to come and spend some time with friends and family because the coming weeks were going to be tough. Nonstop mixtape promotion, interviews, touring, day after day after day. One of the main things he told me to do while I was here was unwind. *Soak up*

all the positive energy from your hometown as you can, he'd said. *That energy brought you here. And it's what will keep you sane. Go barbecue with your daddy, watch a baseball game with your fiancé, because your life is about to change and you're never going to get those normal moments again.*

But what La'Renz didn't understand was that my life had never been normal. My daddy once beat me with an iron, and me and Archie never watched baseball—we sold drugs together our entire relationship.

"Are you Kirbie Amor?"

I turned and saw a guy that looked a few years older than me standing a few respectful paces back. He was wearing a flat-billed KU ballcap cocked so high I could see the start of his hairline. He had a nice smile and keen brown eyes, as if he was eager to come closer to me.

"You know me?" I asked.

"I've been listening to your music since your first song with Coras Bane."

"Oh okay."

"Now you're on Revolt and singing National Anthems. You blew up!"

I smiled. "Not quite."

"You know, I never liked Mary Moét. I used to tell people all the time that she was biting yo style and not giving you credit for it."

The mention of Mary Moét just flipped my mood upside down. I hadn't thought of her in a long time, probably because I was experiencing so much good in my life. I regretted murdering her more than ever now. I acted on hatred, shooting her at almost point blank range simply because she tried to steal my image. Now, in her death, she had become a part of my image and would remain a part for the rest of my life.

The fan asked for a selfie with me and I obliged, giving him a friendly hug afterwards. Then I grabbed my backpack off the carousel and headed to the front of the terminal, where Archie was waiting with a dozen roses. I thanked him, we kissed, and then he held my door open for me as I got in his rental car, a black Chevy Acadia. It was the type of low-key vehicle we used to hustle out of.

"So you think you're a star now, huh?" he said to me when we were driving away from the airport. He said it with a small smile that was less of his normal belittling of my music path and more of a respect for it.

Finally, I thought. *Some respect.*

I grinned. "I've always been a star."

"But who made you a star?"

"Not you."

"Who else put you on yo feet but me?"

"Archie, you know you always hated that I wanted to be a singer."

"I was giving you tough love. I was conditioning you, making that pretty skin of yours extra thick. I put that meat on you, nobody else did. You should be thanking me."

"Thank you, Archie," I said with sarcasm.

"The only thing I didn't like was how close you were to that nigga Coras. In all my years in these streets I can spot a backstabber when I see one. He's waiting to sink it in me deep."

"No he's not."

"He is too. And I didn't like how you invited that nigga to New York before me. I saw those pictures on The Site. I'm your fiancé. Why didn't I get an invitation?"

"Coras coming out there was work-related."

"I don't care."

"Well, me and La'Renz are in Atlanta now. You can come down there to support me at my mixtape release party."

"Is Coras gonna be there?"

"Yes. He's featured on the mixtape."

Archie grunted.

I asked him to take me by my dad's house and he did, but he said he wasn't coming in and I didn't expect him to after their last argument.

My dad answered the door, looking past me at Archie sitting in car, then he let me inside.

"You brought that piece of shit over here with you," said my father, as he locked the door behind me. He had hardly ever cursed since he'd found his faith in God.

"Archie's not coming in," I told him.

"I know he's not."

"I just stopped by to see you before I head back out of town. My first real tour is coming up."

His eyes got wide. "A tour?"

My dad didn't have a social media account so he didn't know what I had been up to. We sat down on the couch in the living room and I updated him about everything from me first meeting La'Renz and Sundi at JFK, to my interview at Revolt that me and La'Renz got kicked out of because La'Renz hit a host named Liam Bashor over the head with a microphone. I told him about the producers I worked with too (leaving out the attempted rape from Timbuck), and I saved the best for last—my National Anthem performance and meeting Caylene Hope.

He stopped me before I could finish. "You met Caylene Hope?" he asked suspiciously.

"You don't believe me?" I said.

"I do. But did you mention me?"

"I told her you're a fan."

"Did you tell her I love her?"

"No ... was I supposed to?"

He sat back against the couch and stared across the room at nothing, lost in a thought that awoke a slight smile. I didn't want to interrupt him, but I had questions that needed answers.

"Daddy, can I ask you something?"

He nodded absentmindedly.

I turned in my seat, facing him. He smiled at me and told me he was proud of me and I thanked him, then said, "That time you and Archie got into an argument, you said something to him that I've been wanting to ask you about."

"I meant every word I said about that punk."

"It's not what you said about him. It's what you said *to* him." I touched my daddy's ear, squeezing his earlobe between my fingers softly. "You said that mom has been one of the most successful women in the music world for the last sixteen years. Who were you talking about?"

He sighed, then rubbed his whole face in frustration. He left his hand over his eyes, hiding himself.

I took his hand away and made him face me. "Daddy, it's time you tell me exactly who she is. I need to know."

He stood up and went to the kitchen—and I followed behind him closely, angrily. As he poured himself a glass of vodka, he said, "I told you who your mother was. She was a good woman who got tired of my abuse. She ran away and never came back. It's my fault, not hers. Don't blame her, blame me."

"Why did you say she was in the music industry?"

He brought the alcohol to his lips and I snatched the glass and poured it into the sink. He wasn't relapsing on my watch.

"Answer me," I said.

"Kirbie, I don't know why I said that. I was just angry."

"Stop lying!"

He looked away from me.

I said, "Are you protecting her? If so, why from me? Is she somebody important?"

"I haven't heard from her in years, Kirbie. I don't know what she's doing with her life."

I could see the falsehoods in my father's eyes, and it brought me on the verge of tears. My phone rang then, and when I checked it I saw it was Archie calling. So I grabbed the bottle of vodka my father had poured from and emptied it all into the sink.

"I'll find out without your help," I said, then turned and headed for the door, throwing the bottle in the trash on my way out. "Bye, daddy."

***

I sat in the passenger seat as Archie drove the rental. I was trying to figure out why my father would be protecting Caylene Hope. The only thing I could come up with was that he was protecting her career. If people found out she had a daughter that she abandoned, then her pro-womanhood public persona would be tarnished. And thus my father would be responsible for crushing her yet again (this time not physically, but it could still hurt her just the same).

For that reason, I was okay with the world not knowing the truth. I would keep the secret.

But I damn sure needed to know.

I was so deep into my thoughts that I barely noticed that we had pulled over on Prospect Avenue in front of a few storefronts. I looked to my left, past Archie, and saw a man in a black barber's pullover shirt jogging across the street toward us. Archie clicked our vehicle's unlock button, and the man climbed in the back seat of our GMC. I looked at the building that the man had come out of. It was a one-level structure called The Fade Factory. It was a barbershop.

A barber had joined us. I looked over at Archie curiously, but he ignored me.

"You'll find what you need under the seat, my nigga," Archie said to our guest with finality. "Put the money under there after you check the package."

"I don't need to check it," said the barber. "You've always done me right. Wussup, Kirbie?"

I looked back at him and paused a second to see if I recognized him—I didn't—before saying hi back. I watched him shove a stack of cash under the seat.

"I like how you're representing the town," the barber said to me after he opened the back door, one foot hanging out. "I wish you the best of luck in that singing shit. It's dope how you sing about selling dope and you really do this shit. Just don't

give the people too much info about the game, you hear me? Don't get yo'self locked up."

"I won't," I smiled. I liked this guy. "What's your name?"

"Kipp Mayor da Barber."

I shook his hand. "Nice to meet you, Kipp."

"You got my support," he said. "Ask Archie. When he told me his girl got a record deal, I told him I'ma buy every disc she put out, the regular and the deluxe versions."

I laughed. "Thank you."

"I'll see you on the next round, Archie."

Kipp hopped out the car, shut the door and jogged back across the street to his shop.

When we pulled off, I turned to Archie. "We've been driving around this whole time with cocaine under the seat?"

He gave me a sideways glance. "When do we not have drugs on us? We're always hustling. Ain't shit changed."

"Yes, it has. I'm starting to become known. More and more people are recognizing me so I can't be around the packages like that. That's not smart, don't you think?"

"I've been moving more weight since you did that Revolt interview. Everybody wants to fuck wit' me now that they know you're my fiancé. I wanted Kipp to see you, to let him know that I'm not lying about you. You're good marketing."

"Archie, at least let me know when we're riding dirty."

"If I do, then what? You're not gonna ride wit' me? Kirbie, we're in this together. We're gonna be married soon. Don't try to change up on me now. We need this money, and you're gonna help me get it. I don't see that music shit bringing in no checks."

I started to mention the $25,000 business check La'Renz wrote to me. But unfortunately La'Renz took it back and hadn't returned it yet. And without physical proof, Archie would think I was getting played. I had my own suspicions lately and I didn't need Archie exacerbating them.

"It takes time to see money," I said. "This music is an investment."

"So is this dope. And it's the only thing giving us returns right now, so I don't want no lip."

I wasn't the nervous type when it came to guns and drugs, but I was uncomfortable now. I didn't want to lose my opportunity with La'Renz and Sundi and Taylor Music Group. Even with my reservations about La'Renz's honesty, I at least wanted a chance to see my mixtape released commercially.

Archie made another drop, this time to a guy I had sold to before. I counted the money for Archie after the guy left, like old times, as Archie cruised toward a Grandview car wash where our next customer was waiting. It went smooth, like it always had since I started hustling with him. I found myself loosening up, weighing packs with the digital scale to make sure Archie was staying sharp (he hit a bump in the round on purpose, and the pack fell down my shirt and we both laughed hysterically). Two hours in the streets and I was looking forward to our next destination, enjoying my old stomping grounds.

"Looks like you're feeling better," Archie said.

I smiled. "I've been away for a while. Forgot how much I missed hustling."

"It's in you. It's all you know."

When me and Archie finally got home, I felt all the stress from my out-of-town work slide off my shoulders. I grew up in this house, with Archie, since the age of fourteen. It was comforting to my soul being here.

He cooked me a plate of baked tilapia with shrimp and spicy calamari served hot. So hot I had to nibble on edges until it cooled. I was licking my fingers during the whole meal, and it made him ask me if La'Renz had been feeding me. "All we ate was hotel food or fast food. A lot of vending machine food too," I told him. "We were always on the go." Afterwards, he took me upstairs by the hand and laid me down on our old California king bed, the sheets puffing out a sweet burst of citrus fabric softener as soon as my back touched. I could tell Archie missed me because he took his time kissing me all over my body, even licking inside the shell of my ear.

A minute or so after we were both naked and Archie started doing me hard, my mind began to wander. Maybe it was the monotony of his grunts that made me drift, I wasn't sure. But I was realizing again that I had never been with another man, yet this time I was *fearing* my curiosity because I wanted to act on it. I allowed myself to think of Julian Beltrán, of how he whispered in my ear, *Farewell, novia ... En otra vida*. I could almost feel his breath tickling my ear. I shuddered.

"Oh yeah," Archie panted. "I missed this pussy …"

I thought of Coras, who had sexually violated me in the studio (amazing!), with Ashleigh looking on (which made it even more unforgettable!), then cornered me on the hotel balcony in Manhattan.

His kisses were so new and fulfilling, his grip so tight and protective.

I moaned.

"I love you, Kirbie," Archie said between sweat-drenched thrusts.

Then I thought of La'Renz Taylor, even though I'd had enough of him over the past few weeks. His dick was monstrous in my mind now, and I was replaying him stepping out of the shower naked over and over again, his meat swinging in constant repeat, back and forth as languid as a pendulum clock, until the loop ended with him climbing on top of me—and me letting him.

I wrapped my arms around Archie's neck.

But La'Renz made me cum.

Monifa Chavis: Having a dinner date with "CB" at Olive Garden in Lee's Summit. All of you haters who loved seeing me single and miserable like you, this Bud's for you! Lol!

CHAPTER 17

Ashleigh Hedgman
Olathe, Kansas

I was so excited after I hung up the phone with promoter Jason Carell, I fell back on my bed as if it were eight inches of snow underneath me, spreading my arms out like a kid making a snow angel. I'd finally booked Coras a gig in Kansas City! It wasn't the Sprint Center but it was the next best thing—a popular nightclub on the southside of town that he'd sold out in the past.

I thought of waiting and surprising him over dinner at Fogo de Choa on the Plaza, but I knew I wouldn't be able to wait that long. I sat up in bed and dialed his number.

He didn't answer. I called back. No answer again.

I realized I didn't have a clue where he was. He had asked to take my Porsche a few hours ago but he should have been back by now. Was he at the studio? Not likely. The only time he stayed gone in my car this early in the evening was when he used to sell weed. But he'd stopped hustling when he fell out with Milo.

Hadn't he?

I suddenly started to wonder. The past couple days Coras hadn't asked me for money at all, not cash, not my credit or debit card that was linked to the account with his show profits, not a dime. I thought I made sure he didn't have access to money unless he asked me first. Did he find a new weed connect and didn't tell me? Or did he go back to Milo?

Before I let my mind get infested with negatives, I texted Coras: *Call me asap. I have good news!* After another twenty minutes waiting for a response I texted Gee Beats: *Tell Coras to call me please. Thank you.* I got an immediate reply from Gee that read: *He's not with me.*

"Hmm ..." I mumbled, dumbfounded.

Where is my man?

The only other way I knew to get a hold of him was through The Site. So I left him a message in his inbox, then scrolled through my newsfeed idly as I waited for his reply. I came across a recent post from Monifa Chavis broadcasting to the world that

she was out to eat with her man—someone with the initials *CB*—at Olive Garden in Lee's Summit. Being curious, especially since Coras's rapper initials were CB, I clicked to her page and read her second most recent status where she claimed she'd reunited with a former love. It was posted a few days ago—which was around the same time Coras stopped asking me for money.

My womanly instincts started to pulse. Something inside of me was telling me to investigate further.

I walked downstairs and peeked out the living room curtains. Yep, my Porsche was still gone. So I went with my first idea and called OnStar and asked them to geo-track my vehicle.

"Is it stolen?" the female operator asked me.

"I don't know yet," I said.

It didn't take her long to locate it. She said, "Your Porsche is in Lee's Summit right now. Where are you? Do you want me to sound its alarm so you can find it?"

My heart started to race. Monifa posted that she was in Lee's Summit. My worst nightmare was coming true!

"I'm in Olathe right now," I answered quickly. "Sounding the alarm won't do a damn thing for me."

"Oh, I'm sorry. I thought you might have forgot where you parked. We get a lot of those."

"Can you pinpoint exactly in Lee's Summit where it's parked?"

"Yes, ma'am. I have it up on my screen already. It's parked in the parking lot of an Olive Garden."

I dropped my cell phone.

***

I stayed calm, or as calm as I could considering my crisis. I had cried for almost two hours, but when Coras called and said he was on his way here, my tears went away and I began to think with a level head. Everything could be explained rationally. One of my college professors taught me this, and I lived by it.

Why would Coras go back to Monifa?

Simple. He missed his independence, having his own money, and Monifa was the link to Milo—that is, his independence.

Whose fault was it that Coras went back to her?

It was my own fault, and I was willing to admit this to Coras as soon as he got home. I had been too controlling. He was a man, and men were leaders, and I was willing to back off and let him lead.

I was willing to do whatever it took to keep Monifa at bay.

My stomach pressed against the bathroom sink as I leaned close to the mirror, combing my straight dark hair. I didn't like the redness in my eyes so I used my eye drops, then I traced on more Chanel eyeliner—thin, precise swipes of the brush along my lashes so Coras would never know I was crying.

Rational men needed strong women.

Then I walked downstairs with grace and sat on my couch, crossing my legs. I intertwined my fingers and set them on my knee. And waited.

A moment or two passed and I heard loud hiphop music outside my house. I stayed put and listened. I almost got upset that Coras was blasting a song sang by Kirbie in my Porsche, in front of my house, but I quickly contained the enmity rising up inside my chest by taking several deep breaths. All it ever took was proper breathing and a fundamental shift in thinking to do away with bad feelings, my professor once said.

When I heard the music and the engine cut off, I got a little nervous. But I remained somewhat calm. *Refrain from yelling at him,* I said to myself. *Don't be ghetto. He expects that behavior from Monifa's type. Be the intelligent, sophisticated woman you were raised to be.*

Ten minutes went by and Coras still hadn't knocked on my front door. I waited another moment then went to the window blinds and peeked out, saw my Porsche sitting in my driveway safely—but no Coras.

Worried, I grabbed my cell phone and called him. He answered right away.

"Coras, where are you?" I said with concern, no spite in my tone whatsoever.

"I'm in traffic," he said.

"Huh? But my Porsche is out front."

"I dropped it off. The keys are in your mailbox. No need for you to call the police."

"Police? Coras, what are you talking about?"

"Look, Ashleigh. I know you saw what Monifa posted. When I called you and told you I was on my way home, I could tell you had been crying. I'm sure you figured out who CB was. You're a smart chick. I didn't want you to find out like that. Monifa was wrong for posting that shit and I told her she was wrong."

"Coras, find out what? Please, just come back home and talk to me. I'm not mad at you."

"Nah, I'm not coming home. I already know you got some bullshit waiting on me and that's what I'm trying to avoid."

"Hang up on her," I heard Monifa say in the background.

Her voice caused every muscle in my upper body to hatefully contract at once, my hand squeezing the phone as if it was her throat. She had no right to give my man directions!

"I gotta go," Coras said to me, and I sat forward on the couch, mouth agape in shock that he would actually listen to her. He'd told me not even a month ago that he wished he would have never fooled around with Monifa, that cutting her off was the best decision he ever made in his life. What was going on here? This can't be happening to me!

"No, Coras, I'm calm! I swear I am! Let's talk about this. I've been there for you since forever. I deserve a face-to-face if you're breaking up with me for Monifa. But you don't need her, I promise! I'll make whatever changes you want me to make. You can have my credit cards. I'll put my house in your name so you'll never have to worry about me threatening to kick you out ever again."

He didn't respond right away, and I got hopeful that he was reconsidering his idiotic decision to choose Monifa over me. *I mean, c'mon, really? Monifa? Uneducated versus educated and independent—who wouldn't choose me?*

"Coras, just come home. This is where you need to be and you know it," I said. "Coras, I'm sorry if I've been a bad manager. Coras? Hello?"

We had gotten disconnected somehow. I called him back but he didn't answer. I kept calling, until the tenth try when I got the realization that it wasn't a dropped call, he wasn't in a dead zone—he had hung up in my face.

I sat on the couch looking at my phone as tears flowed down my cheeks. I closed my eyes and tried to use the power of thought—a technique my professor taught me—to "see" Coras calling me back and confessing his mistake.

But the longer I meditated, the more I felt my sanity slipping away ...

Ashleigh Hedgman > Coras Bane: I'm only using this form of communication because you won't answer my calls. You know I never use The Site to contact you and I never have made our business public until now. I'm desperate, **@CorasBane**. And I don't care who knows it. I need you, baby! Don't give in to that old life. Resist! Monifa is the devil! Don't sell your soul to her! COME HOME! PLEASE!

CHAPTER 18

Kirbie Amor
Kansas City, Missouri

"Where's Coras?" I asked Gee, as I slung my backpack off my shoulder onto the floor. I sat down next to him at his workstation.

"He's not coming," Gee said, then took a sip of his Jack Daniels.

"Dammit. Why?"

He shrugged, then touched a knob on his mixer and a preset clap emerged, adding a thickness to his work-in-progress. He seemed as bummed out as me that Coras wasn't showing up.

Coras didn't know I was in town. I wanted to surprise him. Gee was supposed to call him and tell him to come to the studio, and when he got here I was going to hide under the workstation and scare him by grabbing his leg when he sat down. Gee was going to record it on his smartphone, and if we got

a funny enough reaction we were going to upload it to The Site and see how many Likes we could get.

"Did he say why he couldn't come?" I asked.

"Nope."

"That sucks. He ruined the surprise."

I got my phone out and dialed the first two digits of his number (my smartphone automatically did the rest for me). Clearing my throat in preparation to disguise my voice, I wondered if he'd instantly know it was me. I probably shouldn't have been so excited to see him again but I was. I'd be fooling myself if I thought he wouldn't try something sexual again—I was actually looking forward to what he'd come up with this time. I'd stop him, of course, before he tried to go too far—I was still engaged to be married, you know—but a part of me sort of wanted things to get out of hand.

Oddly, my call was sent to Coras's voicemail. I hadn't listened to his voicemail in so long I had forgotten that he had our mixtape collab playing as his message prompt. I listened merrily until the *beep* came, then left him a voicemail and hung up and tried him again. No answer. Our song replayed. I hung up this time before it finished.

The next best thing was The Site. I logged in and typed in his name with my thumb and clicked the link that took me to his profile page. I was going to leave him a private message in his inbox, but I was stopped by a vehement comment posted to his page by Ashleigh. I couldn't believe what I was reading. If this was real, then Coras had left Ashleigh for Monifa.

What the fuck?

I clicked on the sub comments of Ashleigh's crazy post. It was back-and-forth drama between Ashleigh and Monifa.

>**Monifa Chavis:** See, I knew something had been going on between you two. I knew you were more than his manager. I'm watching out for Kirbie when I should've been watching out for you! But you can delete this post because Coras is done with you.
>
>**Ashleigh Hedgman:** The only reason he's with you is for your brother's drugs. How long do you think that's gonna last? When all you fuckers go to jail I'm gonna bond Coras out and he's gonna come back home where he's supposed to be!
>
>**Monifa Chavis:** Stop talking reckless on The Site, you retard! My brother doesn't sell drugs.
>
>**Ashleigh Hedgman:** Everybody in KC knows what your brother does. And don't comment under my

posts if you don't want to hear the truth, bitch! This post was for my man. Stay your fucking ghetto ass out of it.

Monifa Chavis: He's not your man anymore Lol! And don't mention my name in a post and maybe I will stay out of it. And by the way, nice Porsche. The leather seats were comfy lol!

Ashleigh Hedgman: I'm gonna snatch you by your hair and punch your face in, bitch! We're gonna see how many lols you got after that! Wait till I see you, bitch!

Monifa Chavis: So who's the ghetto one now? I would respond to your threat but I have class. Lol!

I was so disappointed in Coras. How could he go back to Monifa and get tied back in with Milo after what Milo's goon did to Gee? That was betrayal.

I showed Gee my phone. "Have you seen this bullshit?" I asked him.

Gee looked at my display screen while sipping his drink. He nodded.

"You knew Coras was back with Monifa?" I said incredulously.

"Yeah. He told me."

"And you approved?"

Gee shrugged one shoulder. "He said Milo doesn't fuck with the dude who shot me no more. I understand what Coras is doing. He gotta eat. He was going through it with Ashleigh."

"I don't give a fuck what he was going through."

I tried to call Coras again. Surprisingly, he picked up this time.

"Kirbie?" he answered, his voice smiling. "Wussup wit it girl?"

"That's what I'm trying to figure out. What the hell is this shit I'm seeing on The Site?"

He explained in one word. "Drama," he said.

"You're back with Monifa?!"

"For the time being."

"That's fucking unacceptable, Coras! Milo is responsible for nearly having Gee killed. You're sleeping with the enemy!"

"I already talked to Gee about it. He knows what's going on. He's cool with it."

"Of course he's gonna be cool with it. That's how Gee is. He goes with the flow because he's your homeboy. But real niggas don't do their homeboys how you're doing Gee."

"So I'm not a real nigga now?"

"I didn't say that. But what you're doing isn't real shit. You're selling out for cash."

His voice rose. "Look, Kirbie. Some of us still have to get it how we live. Not everybody has the luxury to fly all around the country—New York, Atlanta—doing celebrity interviews and singing National Anthems and shit. Some of us still gotta get it out the mud. Don't hate me because I'm still grittin'. You don't have no idea what I'm going through because you're hundreds of miles away in music land."

I said, "Actually, I'm in Kansas City *right now*."

He got quiet for a moment, then said, "You're at Gee's studio?"

"Yes. Where are you?"

He paused again, and that let me know that he was either out hustling or cuddled up with Monifa.

"I'ma call you later," he said. "How long are you gon' be in town?"

"You better not fucking hang up on me!"

"I wasn't gon' hang up."

"The Coras I know wouldn't wait till later. He would drop everything and pull up right now. We used to be a solid team. Swope Records till death, remember?"

"C'mon, Kirbie, don't try and hit me with that shit. Just a little while ago you said fuck Swope Records and ran off with your fiancé to do the same thing I'm doing now. Hustling, grittin'. So who are you to judge me? Don't be a hypocrite."

I nearly hung up on Coras right then. But we never hung up on each other, no matter how mad we got.

"Bye, Coras," I said.

"Bye, Kirbie. I'll see you later."

"No, you won't."

"Yes, I will."

"Bye. I'm hanging up."

"A'ight, bye."

A half hour after me and Coras talked, I was standing in the booth alone, studio headphones tight on my ears, waiting for the intro chords of Gee's new instrumental to fade and the downbeat to drop in. I had written a song vowing to never let a man (Coras) sexually touch me again, especially while that man (Coras) was using other women for financial gain.

CHAPTER 19

La'Renz "Buddy Rough" Taylor
Atlanta, Georgia

Sundi's uber-soft lips tugged on the foreskin of my hard dick with just the right amount of pull—the best head I had received since I'd been out of prison, by far. I was leaning against the dresser in the hotel as she kneeled before me sucking and bobbing away like she had a point to prove. I looked down at her and rubbed my fingers through her hair.

"I don't feel worthy of this, Sundi," I said. "This is too good for a lonely old man like me."

She made a noise out of her nostrils similar to a giggle, without even the slightest pause in head movement. Then she took a hold of my dick and balls and placed spongy kisses on the surface skin near my anus. She knew what I liked and disliked—she was playing with my boundaries.

"You're not old," she said, as she squeezed the base of my member, cutting of circulation while licking my tip. "And there's no such thing as too good."

Actually, there is, I thought.

Where another man might've been thankful for an enthralling dicksuck from such a beautiful young woman like Sundi, I was leaning more toward curiousness and cynicism. She wasn't this good when I went to prison. Seven years ago I had to teach her about sensitivity, about the "sweet spots" of my erection and how feather-light licking could be more stimulating than jerking and slobbering. She thought it was funny that a man named Buddy Rough had a preference for tender loving care.

Since then, she'd clearly had practice.

My question was: *With whom?*

But it was a question I didn't want to know the answer to, at least not right now, not while she was unearthing feelings of pleasure I hadn't felt in years.

On the verge of cumming in her mouth, I stood her up and sat her on the dresser. I pushed inside of her and she gasped with her chin to the sky, wrapping her legs around me and locking her ankles. I seized her neck between my teeth, nibbling and sucking, feeling the warmth of her blood flow through her jugular veins. I wanted to come inside of her while holding her close, and that's what I did.

"I love you, Buddy Rough," she moaned afterwards, still holding me.

"I love you too, Sundi." I stared at the bite marks I'd left in her throat and took my thumb and tried to massage them out.

She lifted her chin for me. "Is it bad?" she asked.

"No, it's not that bad. I don't think so. I'm sorry, Sundi. I was caught up in the moment and—"

"Don't apologize, La'Renz." She smiled, then lifted her right breast and showed me the traces of her dark brown scar. She pointed to it with her other hand. "As long as you don't do *this* again, you can do whatever you want to do to me during sex." She laughed.

I laughed too. "You got a deal," I said. "No more war wounds."

I went to the bed and sat down as she walked to the bathroom. I felt winded. I felt old. Looking down at my flaccid penis, I could see that Sundi's juices had lathered my shaft completely. Some of it had already started to crust. I thought back to the moment when I walked out of the shower naked in front of Kirbie. I smiled to myself. Around the time when I first met Jazzmine, I did the same thing. Jazzmine stared at my length and girth and uttered, "Nice," with wide eyes. And even though Kirbie didn't say a thing when she saw me nude, her facial expression spoke volumes. She was beyond impressed; she was captivated.

Now every time Kirbie thought of sex, I was certain she'd think of me.

"What is this?" Sundi asked.

I looked up and saw Sundi holding a thick 9x12 manila envelope, its gummed flap fully sealed. "I don't know what it is," I said as she handed it to me. "Where'd you get it?"

"Somebody shoved it under the front door as I was coming from the bathroom. You get your mail delivered here?"

"No. I have a P.O. Box."

With alarm, I yanked on my slacks one leg at a time and stormed out of the room fastening my belt, looking both ways down the hallway for anybody who might've slid the envelope under my door. I saw an old woman at the end of the hall in fleece jogging pants climbing on the elevator, but before she went inside she paused and glanced back at me teasingly.

"Hey!" I yelled, and started running after her barefoot on the red carpeted floor. "Hey, hold up bitch!"

But by the time I made it down the hall the elevator the doors had closed shut. I smacked the doors with my palm.

"Shit."

I walked back to my room and saw Sundi in the mirror putting her earrings back on.

"Did you find who dropped it off?" she asked.

"No," I said, grabbing the envelope and ripping it open.

"You should call the front desk. I'm sure they know who came up here."

"I doubted."

Anxiously, I pulled the contents out of the envelope. It was full of high-quality black-and-white photographs. At first I didn't know what or who I was looking at—the first picture I studied was an indistinguishable still shot of a man and woman having fierce sex, their fuck faces contorted in rageful ecstasy. But the next picture was a full frame close-up, and the image of the two lovers was tack sharp and recognizable.

I was looking at sex photos of Eliyah Golomb and Sundi Ashworth.

I was so infuriated I started to see red.

"La'Renz, can you help me with my necklace?" Sundi asked me. When she finally turned and saw my facial expression, she frowned. "What's wrong?"

I showed her what was wrong. I threw the photos at her and they floated to the ground at her feet. She squatted to pick one up, then gasped.

She looked up at me in horror. "La'Renz, these are old photos."

"You never told me you fucked Eliyah!" I roared.

"I didn't know I was supposed to."

Wrong answer.

I closed the space between us fast, before she had a chance to shrink away. Then I grabbed a fistful of her hair and yanked her to her feet.

"La'Renz, please!"

She struggled back, so I threw her to the ground near the front door.

"Get the fuck out!" I yelled. "You're a fucking traitor! I should've fuckin' known. "

"La'Renz, what happened between me and Eliyah lasted a short time. It had nothing to do with you." She was crying, mascara running down her cheeks. "I love you. I never loved him."

"Get out, WHORE!"

"Can't you see what Eliyah is trying to do? He's trying to split us apart because he's jealous of you. I never agreed to or even had the slightest idea that he took pictures of us having sex. What he did was illegal, La'Renz. This is a setup."

I took my belt off and wrapped a few inches of it around my fist, letting the slack hang to the floor. "I'm only going to tell you one more time. Get up and get out of my room!"

She stared up at me with eyes full of tears, but didn't move. She was shaking. "La'Renz, you've changed. You're not gonna hit me with that belt because you're not the same person you once were. You can't let Eliyah drive a wedge—"

I swung the belt in a violent arc as hard as I could.

Swap!

She howled in pain. The belt caught her on the thigh, leaving a severe red welt.

I didn't have to tell her to leave again. She scrambled to her feet, fell down, got back up on wobbly legs and gathered her things as quickly as she could. I swung the belt at her again but *swapped* the door as she ran out.

If I wouldn't have missed, I would've gotten her on the neck.

Fuckin' whore, I thought, dropping the belt at my feet. I locked the door and sat down on my bed again, looking down at all the lewd photos strewn about.

Eliyah fucked Sundi.

In some photos he appeared to be fucking her hard, while looking directly into the hidden lens as if he knew I'd see these pictures one day.

Eliyah fucked Sundi.

Eliyah FUCKED Sundi.

That son of a bitch!

It was a painful fact to grasp, so painful I could feel the tears welling in my eyes.

But I knew how to get rid of pain and tears.

After taking a deep breath and closing my eyes tight to fight back the sorrow, I grabbed my cell phone off the nightstand and called Julian Beltrán.

CHAPTER 20

Sundi Ashworth
Atlanta, Georgia

"Bastard!" I cried, as I banged my back against the rear of the elevator car, hiding my face in my palms. My chest was heaving up and down as I bawled my eyes out. "Muthafucking bastard!"

I was infuriated with La'Renz for whipping me. He really hit me! I lifted my dress and stared at the red welt in disbelief. It had already caused irritation of the surrounding blood cells, making the welt look larger than it really was.

But even if I wasn't hurting from physical pain, I was still tormented with anguish. The reality that Eliyah Golomb had been playing me from the beginning struck me hard. He never had any intentions of hiring me back, because he'd been planning for this moment to send La'Renz those pornographic pictures of us since he hired me—*six years ago!*

I had been a pawn in his sick, drawn out beef with La'Renz.

And I allowed it to happen.

As the elevator descended, I tried to take deep breaths and control my sobbing but I couldn't. Black mascara poured down my cheeks, curling under my jowls dripping everywhere.

I felt a small sense of relief when the claustrophobic elevator finally chimed and released me into the parking garage. I walked fast, strutting across the pavement in my high heels as I searched my purse for the keys to my Dodge Charger I rented from the airport. I should have been able to easily find them; they had a yellow tag attached. But what I really should have done was hook them onto my home keys instead of—

Swish. Swish.

I stopped in my tracks and turned around quickly, trying to determine where that noise came from but I didn't see anyone. Just endless rows of forlorn automobiles.

"Hello?" I said. My voice traveled in a broad echo. "Hello?"

No one answered back, but I could have sworn I heard someone walking in a loud pair of fleece pants.

Brushing it off, I kept looking for my keys as I walked, mumbling to myself, "Sundi, you have to start choosing better men. No more men in the music industry. This business is so crooked and conniving, there's no way you'll find a man that hasn't been corrupted by the politics and childish feuds."

At my car, I took another deep reposeful breath and let it out slowly, then stuck my hand in my purse again and finally found my keys in a side pocket.

"Jesus, thank you," I said in relief. Otherwise I would have had to call the rental car company, and who knew how long it would have taken them to get anything done, especially at this time of night.

Swish. Swish-swish-swish.

I turned, this time with cat-like reflexes. But again I saw no one.

"Is anyone there?" I said, the tremor in my tone betraying how scared I was. "I know somebody's there."

The silence was frightening.

"La'Renz?" I looked around, peering over roofs of cars as best I could. "La'Renz, is that you?"

Nervously, I turned back around and tugged on the door handle, which was supposed to unlock by touch as long as you had the key fob nearby. I had it in my hand and it didn't engage! I had no idea why it was malfunctioning.

I tried it again. The handle lifted but stayed locked.

"Fuck!"

I had this same problem at the airport, and the service guy gave me a new fob. He told me if I had this problem again, then just use the traditional key, which was stored inside the fob. In pushing down on the fob's key-retract button, I dropped the whole damn set on the ground. Hastily I bent down to snatch it off the pavement, then bounced back up—and that's when I saw the reflection of the old woman from Eliyah's mansion in my window glass. I screamed.

"Quiet!" she hissed.

Before I could turn around, the woman grasped my head in her hands and violently gave a hard shove forward. My face blasted through my driver's window and glass shattered everywhere, the most excruciating pain I'd ever felt in my life.

It was the last thing I remembered ...

CHAPTER 21

La'Renz "Buddy Rough" Taylor
Atlanta, Georgia

Out front, the valet pulled my rented Lamborghini into the semi-circle of the hotel and brought it to a halt at the curb in front of me. Its canary yellow paint job glistened all over, marvelously, like magic. As it idled, the driver's door lifted vertically into the sky and the young valet hopped out with spunk—as if he'd just had the time of his life—and then handed me the keys.

"There you go, Buddy Rough," he said, smiling. "Drive safe. Oh, and I took a selfie in your Lambo. Is that okay?"

It seemed as if he was going for his phone to maybe show me his photo or take a selfie with me personally, so I pushed past him and dropped down in the driver's seat, pulled my door down and took off.

Vrooom! Scuuurt!

As I traveled south down Pryor Road, I thought about what I'd done to Sundi. I knew I hurt her bad, physically and mentally. But the old me—Buddy Rough in his 30s—would have hurt her a lot worse.

The old me might've killed her.

Shifting into the next gear up, I pictured the sinister smile on Eliyah's face when he was stuffing that envelope with those sexually explicit pictures, sealing it closed with his pitch-forked tongue. I pictured him pouring himself a glass of champagne afterwards, toasting to his own reflection in the mirror with another devilish smile.

"You made your move, Eliyah," I said out loud. "Now it's time for me to make mine."

The Lamborghini's engine howled as I accelerated into my next turn, which was a bend in the main road that took me to a crowded shopping center. My instructions were to pull around back, so I did, barely able to squeeze my Lamborghini between a utility pole and a Ford SUV that had parked too far away from the curb. I came awfully close to scratching one of the sideview mirrors.

As I waited in this back alley, I started to wonder if maybe I shouldn't have driven such an exotic, attention-grabbing vehicle to buy cocaine. But it was short notice and the Lamborghini was what I

had as transportation, so it was either this or do the deal out of a cab.

Before I went to prison, me and Julian Beltrán used to make all of our deals out of either his Los Angeles restaurant or the one he owned in New York City. I told him all the time he needed to also consider building a hub in Atlanta because that was where musicians were flocking to. It made sense because Julian catered to musical artists, producers, music insiders, and celebrities from other fields who needed drugs to cope with the restlessness of high-level success. It seemed like he finally listened to me.

The back door to Julian's restaurant opened and a young Mexican male with a buzz cut waved for me to come on. I knew he was Mexican Mafia because of the tattoos inked on the back of his hand that disappeared up his sleeve.

I got out, closed the door but didn't even lock it. I didn't care if someone stole it or anything inside. Quite frankly, I didn't give a shit about anything right now except crushing Eliyah Golomb.

"You need to wear this blindfold," the young Mexican said.

"I don't wear blindfolds, my friend," I replied. "*No bueno.*"

"If you're here then you know the rules. No blindfold, no access."

"You must not recognize me. My name's La'Renz 'Buddy Rough' Taylor. I'm partners with Julian."

"Do you know how many celebrities come to this back door throwing their names around like I give a fuck?"

"Unlike them, I'm a dealer not a user."

"Rules are rules, *mi amigo*. Blindfold—put the damn thing on."

I looked the kid square in the eyes. He was probably just starting high school when I went to prison.

He held the blindfold out. Reluctantly, I took it from him. But I didn't tie it around my eyes. I stuffed it inside the crotch of my Tom Ford slacks and rubbed my balls with it real good, then pulled it out and threw it in the kid's face.

"You wear it," I said.

In a rage, he bounced out of the doorway and grabbed my dress shirt by the chest as if he thought he could easily man-handle me. He managed to shove me backwards up against my Lambo, but now that I had back support, I was able to push off and elbow him across the jaw.

It was a solid hit.

And in the split-second that it took him to rethink and re-strategize his stupid decision to attack me in the first place, I grabbed his shoulders for leverage and gut-checked him with a knee. It hurt him so bad he actually dropped down to all fours. I hooked an arm around his neck from behind and picked him up in the same motion, choking him. Squeezing. Choking him harder.

"I bet you're gonna remember me next time," I growled in his ear. "La'Renz 'Buddy Rough' Taylor. The Mogul."

With the kid being relatively young, I surmised that the range of motion in his neck was too limber, and there was no way I'd be able to snap it. Not that I would have tried it on one of Julian's soldiers, but the thought did occur to me.

"Let ... me ... go," he wheezed, using way too much air that, if I was in his position, I would have tried to save.

When I saw several more tattooed mafia members storm out the back door—all of them armed with firearms of different calibers and barrel lengths—I let the kid go immediately and pushed him away from me. If this group of criminals lived by the same creed as Julian's old bunch, then they would've shot through the kid just to kill me.

"Still haven't lost that temper, have you?" said Julian Beltrán, who had just stepped out the back door to join his men. He walked up to the kid I had choked—the kid was still breathing hard like a bull, staring at me like he wanted to charge me again—and patted the kid on the shoulder to get him to calm down. The kid stepped back in line with the rest of the men, then Julian approached me with his hand extended, wearing a smile that said he wasn't surprised I'd gotten into a fight. "I just knew it was you out here causing a ruckus. I don't know whether to shake your hand or shoot you."

I tucked the tail of my dress shirt back in my slacks, then shook his hand. "He wanted me to wear a blindfold. When'd you start that shit?"

***

The meeting with Julian was fun. It felt like old times, except now his restaurant's food actually tasted good. We worked out a deal that would provide me enough cocaine to supply a few famous people I knew that still got high, and that was all I needed—for now. Apparently, Julian had nabbed

a few millionaire customers I used to deal to, thus shouldering me out of that cashflow. But what could I do? I was in prison; they had to get their dope from somewhere. But thankfully I still had some rich friends who snorted a line on occasion who would never deal with the Mexican Mafia directly.

And that guaranteed that Julian Beltrán would always need me.

As I launched the Lamborghini down a continual stretch of highway in the dark of night, I glanced to the east where I could barely see my hotel amid other tall, glowing buildings. I passed by its exit—and several other exits, continuing on my quest south of downtown Atlanta—trying to figure out how Eliyah Golomb had known that I was staying in that particular hotel room. He'd narrowed me down to that very room somehow.

Details like that would haunt me if let them, so for the moment I tried not to wonder about how he found me. I turned up an un-mastered song off of Kirbie's upcoming mixtape, cranked it to the max and was bummed that it wouldn't go up any more. I was twenty minutes out from Hartsfield-Jackson Atlanta International Airport, where I was picking up Kirbie. I really needed her company right now after what happened between me and Sundi.

"You're all I got left, Kirbie," I said to myself in the loneliness of my Lamborghini.

One hand on the wheel, I reached into the inside pocket of my suit jacket and pulled out a small pack of cocaine. It was a sample I had requested from Julian. The fashion-savvy Beltrán Cartel leader called me out on it too, saying he'd already gave me a sample pack not long after my first day of freedom. But I lied and said I lost it, when in all actuality I had cut it open and washed it down Sundi's kitchen sink because I didn't want to disappoint her.

But now Sundi had no stake in my decision-making.

I got to the airport with time to spare. Kirbie's flight wasn't scheduled to arrive for another half hour. I drove under a couple overstreet walkways, then pulled over in a no-parking zone and turned on my hazard lights.

I examined the pack of cocaine in both hands like it was a gold bar.

"This is what will give you control over the industry again," I said. "Drug dealing is the one advantage you have over Eliyah. You just can't let it control you this time. All things should be done in moderation."

I opened up the plastic and sniffed a moderate pinch of cocaine off my fingernail. Instantly, bold sensations seemed to replenish my aged insides, giving me a feeling of youthful euphoria. I leaned my head back against the headrest and smiled.

Wow, I thought.

Then I reached in my glove box and grabbed one of my business cards, used it to scoop up a larger sample of coke (larger, but still moderate compared to what I used to snort back in the day) and sniffed it into my opposite nostril in one big face-twisting drag.

The high was nothing short of amazing.

Satisfied, I started up the Lamborghini and followed the airport signs to Kirbie's terminal. All I could think about was what kind of sexy jeans she'd be stepping off the plane in—and how long it would take me to get between her pretty little legs.

GabbyTV: BUDDY ROUGH STRIKES AGAIN! Reports are out that La'Renz 'Buddy Rough' Taylor physically assaulted his former mistress Sundi Ashworth, leaving her hospitalized in an Atlanta medical center. The motive behind the assault is alleged to have stemmed from sin-filled JEALOUSY! Apparently La'Renz didn't like the fact that Sundi has been boinking music mogul Eliyah Golomb since he went away to prison, so the ex-con bashed her head through her car window. And yes I have proof *(see link below)* that Sundi has been sleeping with Eliyah. Exclusive pictures were sent to me anonymously that clearly show the two doing the do. And in a statement from Eliyah Golomb himself, he stated that he's "deeply embarrassed" by the photos of him exposing all his glory, therefore authenticating them. Now before you all start calling Sundi a ho again, let me put it out there that she's currently in a coma and we all need to keep her in our prayers. She's the victim here. As they say, *For with what judgment ye judge, ye shall be judged.* Let's hope this applies to La'Renz's ass too.

GabbyTV Exclusive—>Click here for exclusive nude pics of Sundi Ashworth!

CHAPTER 22

Sammy "The Hitman" Russtrip
Brooklyn, New York

"She could have tried to kill Sundi a thousand different ways," I explained to Eliyah, who was sitting near me at the head of the conference table in the east corner of his mansion. "The human body is inexplicably resilient. Its core programming is first and foremost survival, and the body will shut down and reboot over time to ensure survival. So for Rose to think a mere beat down would finish Sundi Ashworth off ... I just think it was foolish, amateur, and short-sighted. She took no post-attack checks to make sure her vic was dead."

"I did too!" Rose shouted. The old Spanish woman was sitting across from me, to Eliyah's left, her baggy eyes fixed on me in a venomous rage. Even though Eliyah gave me the floor, I knew she wouldn't be able to hold her tongue. We were the only three in this room. "I checked her pulse and

I didn't feel one," she said. "I thought the girl was dead."

"There's more than one way to check for life."

"I didn't have time to try anything else. We were in a parking garage. People come and go and I had to get out of there."

"Then you shouldn't have attacked her," I countered.

"What gives you the right to question me?"

"I have never made an attempt on a target's life and had one survive."

"Me either, till now."

"Somehow I doubt that."

"Sundi is practically dead!" Rose shouted.

"The recovery rate of people who enter a comatose state due to injury of the cerebral cortex is relatively high. Rose, you're old enough to know that it's a good chance she'll pull through."

"Fuck you, bastard!"

"Fuck you too, bitch."

"You're nothing but a big kiss-ass!"

"Cunt."

"¡Me cago en tu puta madre!"

"Right back at'cha."

"Stop it you two!" Eliyah shouted. "Rose, can you step out for a minute so I can have a word alone with Sammy?"

Rose put on her fake, obedient smile and told Eliyah she'd be glad to. Then she stood up and threw me another icy look before storming out of the conference room making all the noise in the world in her fleece jogging pants. *Swish-swish-swish-swish.*

"Why don't you like Rose?" Eliyah asked me after she was gone. He leaned back in his leather executive chair and studied me. He seemed amused.

"I think she's incompetent," I said. "She's trying to hold on to something that she used to be. She's old, and it's evident that her better judgment is cooked. She needs to let go."

"It's hard for all of us to let go of our former selves, don't you think?"

"That's no excuse."

Eliyah nodded in agreement. "But here's my dilemma. I need Rose. I have a lot of *situations* popping up, especially since La'Renz got out of prison, and it's hard keeping up with it all because it's hard finding good help. Unfortunately, you can't be everywhere at once."

"My son Jarvis would have made sure Sundi was dead. And that's allowing that he would've even attacked her in the first place. Rose's orders were to drop off the photographs at La'Renz's hotel room and leave. That's it."

"But La'Renz was supposed to brutally assault Sundi himself upon seeing the pictures. He didn't. And when Rose saw Sundi walk into the parking garage without a scratch on her, she made a judgement call. We can both say that it worked. The media is holding La'Renz responsible."

"But what happens when Sundi wakes up from her coma and identifies Rose?"

"We'll cross that bridge when we get to it."

I sighed. "Rose was wrong. Any real investigator knows that there's only one constant that can be counted on during a mission—and that constant is self. You can't depend on your target to move into your trap. You have to make him move into it. And that takes planning, not improvisation like Rose did. I teach Jarvis this all the time."

"Are you saying that Jarvis is ready to go out on his own?" Eliyah asked. "Is it time to split you two up?"

I pondered on this question for a moment. All I really wanted was for Rose to get fired. Jarvis still needed guidance, his firearm skillset in low-light shooting was mediocre, and his idea of hard work was screwed up—he was too excited about getting his first on-the-job murder but got bored quick with the prep time leading up to it. And too much of his time was spent on that damn smartphone.

However, I was confident that my son could do a better job than Rose.

"Yes," I said to Eliyah. "You could split us up and he'd be fine."

"He's ready?"

"Yes, sir, he's ready."

I brought Eliyah up to speed on all the information I had on his targets. I reminded him that a few weeks back Sundi Ashworth and Thomas Dyer had lunch together, and that this morning Thomas hopped on a flight to Atlanta, Georgia, most likely to visit Sundi in the hospital. I told him that my son Jarvis discovered that La'Renz's artist, Kirbie Amor, was cheating on her back-home fiancé with a local rapper named Coras Bane, that it was information that could be used to reshape her public image if La'Renz succeeded in making her a superstar.

I *didn't* tell him about the time La'Renz came close to walking up on me and Jarvis when we were sitting in the Yukon outside Sundi's townhome. We pulled off before La'Renz discovered us, but the mere mention of it would make me look bad.

Afterwards, I shook Eliyah's hand and was on my way out the door when he stopped me.

"Sammy, I have one more question for you."

I turned to him, stuffing my hands in the back pockets of my brown slacks. "Yes, sir?"

"If things don't pan out like we want them to and I ask you to kill La'Renz Taylor for me, will you be able to do it?"

I frowned. "Yes, sir. Why do you ask?"

"You used to work for him."

"That's true. But I didn't swear an oath to him. My services aren't offered on feelings of obligation due to prior employment or friendship or patriotism or any other silly notion. My services are offered by contract only, in two-year terms. That's how it's always been."

Eliyah looked at me for a moment, then nodded slowly, as if my answer brought him clarity. I thought I saw the faintest of smiles appear on his face. "Okay, Sammy. You're dismissed."

CHAPTER 23

Thomas Dyer
Atlanta, Georgia

I never thought I'd be sitting beside Sundi Ashworth while she laid in a hospital bed with oxygen tubes taped to her, as if she were some kind of experiment gone wrong. It killed me to see her in a coma, fighting for her life.

I leaned forward in my chair, planted my elbows on my knees and brought my fists together and said a silent prayer, begging God to return her to full health. I was on the verge of tears.

And when I opened my eyes and saw her beaten face again, I couldn't hold back; I started to cry.

The cuts and bruises were so pronounced that if you hadn't known Sundi beforehand, you would never have known how beautiful she was.

"Please come out of this, Sundi," I said to her unconscious body. I put my hand on her wrist. She was unresponsive. "Please, Sundi. I have so much

I want to get off my chest, so much to confess to you."

For nearly a decade I had been in love with Sundi Ashworth. No one could possibly know how painful it felt to hold such strong feelings in for someone close for so long. It had been eating me alive. I was going bald because of it. I had to watch her be mistreated by La'Renz Taylor time after time, watch her play second fiddle to Jazzmine Short when she should have never been anybody's second anything. She was a gem, and La'Renz treated her like a prisoner of war.

And now *this*.

The bastard came close to murdering her!

I pulled out my phone and logged into The Site to see if there were any reports that he'd been arrested. But what I found was a trending post from GabbyTV that, in so many words, reduced Sundi to a whore who got what she had coming. I'd seen my fair share of exploitative posts from Gabby throughout her career, but this one was by far the lowest of the low. She even had the audacity to include text from the Bible, and then shared a link to nude photos of Sundi and Eliyah in the same reference.

I didn't click on the pics.

But I did click on the comments.

LaQuisha Day: You can always count on La'Renz to fuck some shit up lol! At least he never disappoints.

VVS Vernon: Eliyah and La'Renz were sharing Sundi Ashworth. I wonder if they shared Jazzmine Short.

Krissy PraiseHim Walker: Why are we ignoring the real problem here? Yes, La'Renz might've went too far in handling things but it takes two to tango. Did Sundi instigate things by sleeping with La'Renz's sworn enemy? What kind of woman is that messy? Sundi isn't as innocent as the media wants us to believe.

Michaela McDonnell: How the fuck did this bitch end up with two multi-millionaires? I can't get ONE nigga to split rent. And my titties look bigger than hers.

Quita Wheeler: Gabby we can always count on you to give us the lowdown. I love u girl!

RaShawn McElroy: @PittyTheFool @ClydeJones Look at these pics of Sundi Ashworth! Oh shit!

PittyTheFool: She got a mean body. I would've tried to kill her too if she cheated on me.

Clyde Jones: Eliyah didn't look like he was hitting that right ijs

Terry's Lovin: I bet Eliyah is gonna take Kirbie from La'Renz next. Eliyah is a Jewish pimp.

Edward RightToBearArms Consentino: Fuck these pictures. Gabby, where's the sex tape?

Rita RealSpit Gibson: We sometimes hold these celebrities to a higher standard because of the influence they have over our young people. But they're human just like all of us. This is proof. We all have to face the consequences of our actions, no matter our status in life. This should be a lesson learned for everybody, not just our youth. Gabby said it best. *For with what judgment ye judge, ye shall be judged.* But she left out the rest of that verse. It says, *And with what measure ye mete, it shall be measured unto you.*

It was happening to Sundi again. She had managed to repair her public image after the scandal between her, La'Renz, and Jazzmine Short, and now La'Renz had managed to ruin it again in less than six months. I promised myself that if Sundi didn't get better soon (and even if she did) I was going to make La'Renz pay for all of his crimes.

He got off easy with prison.

I never understood why Sundi was attracted to La'Renz. How could any woman be drawn to such arrogance, immorality and abusiveness? I told myself that Sundi had just been a young girl dazzled by his money and power, as most girls would be at that age. The spectacle of fame and fortune was hypnotizing. It would explain why she fell for Eliyah Golomb too.

But there had to be something that Sundi saw in me because she just recently invited me to lunch. Maybe she was tired of being under the microscope in relation to men like La'Renz and Eliyah. Maybe she wanted to try out a season of normalcy that she'd find in me.

I stared at her in tears ... *Maybe I'm too late*, I thought.

"*Hm-uhhh!*" Sundi gasped.

It scared the shit out of me when I heard the hard breath she took and saw how her chest heaved, literally arching her spine off the sheets in one contorted spasm.

I catapulted to my feet, leaning over her bed and staring into her face waiting for her to open her eyes. "Sundi, can you hear me? It's me, Thomas."

Then my worst nightmare took form. Her heart monitor flatlined.

Beeeeep!

I ran out into the hall and screamed down the hallway. "Help me! I need a doctor in here! Somebody get a fucking doctor!"

Text **FELONY** to **77948**

And stay updated on all of Felony Books' *newest releases, free giveaways,* and *special promotions!*

Would you like to become a **published author**? We're looking for aspiring authors in the following genres: STREET LIT, ROMANCE, THRILLERS, SUSPENSE, HORROR, and MYSTERY. Complete creative freedom, with 50% royalties! If you have what it takes, submit your first three chapters to:

felonybooks@gmail.com

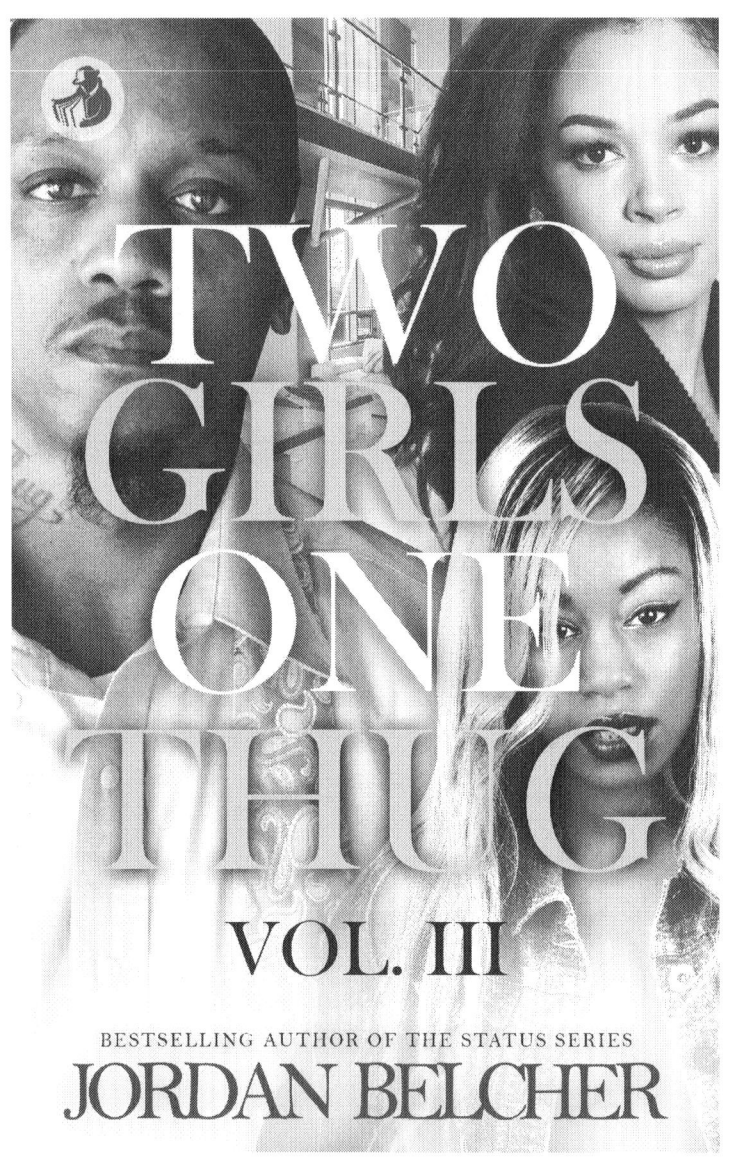

ON SALE NOW!

www.felonybooks.com

ON SALE NOW!

www.felonybooks.com

ON SALE NOW!

www.felonybooks.com

ON SALE NOW!

ON SALE NOW!

www.felonybooks.com

Made in United States
Orlando, FL
15 September 2022